Love's Hidden Treasure

LOVE'S HIDDEN TREASURE

•

KATHY MILLER &
DARLENE JURGENS

AVALON BOOKS
THOMAS BOUREGY AND COMPANY, INC.
401 LAFAYETTE STREET
NEW YORK, NEW YORK 10003

© Copyright 1992 by Kathy Miller and Darlene Jurgens
Library of Congress Catalog Card Number: 92-71137
ISBN 0-8034-8934-X

PRINTED IN THE UNITED STATES OF AMERICA
ON ACID-FREE PAPER
BY HADDON CRAFTSMEN, SCRANTON, PENNSYLVANIA

This book is dedicated to the memory of Darlene's father,
Robert Jurgens, and Kathy's mother, Annie Airey. We wish they
could have shared it with us.

Chapter One

Alyson was overcome with a sense of awe. Never had she seen such rugged beauty—sweeping valleys, lakes tinged an emerald green, snow-capped mountains stretching to the horizon. So this was the lure that had been beckoning her father to return for so many years. At least she could understand that part of him. The rest of the puzzle she held in her hands.

Alyson's eyes were drawn again to the legal documents that named her owner of a piece of this wilderness. Only three months ago had she learned of its existence, after her father's lawyer produced the only item of any value in her father's estate. She could still hear the apology in Mr. Asquith's, "I'm so sorry, Miss Langdon. Your father reinvested his funds four years ago in order to purchase land. It's in a place near the

Arctic Circle . . . I'm sure he must have had some project in mind . . . some future plans.''

Alyson closed her eyes and leaned her head back as the pain of her recent loss washed over her. How she missed her father! How she longed to turn back the clock to spend more time with him! Perhaps he would have shared his future plans with her. The Canadian North had always lured him; she knew that. But to invest all he had in a place so remote, so—

''Excuse me. I believe this is yours.''

Alyson's eyes flew open. For one panic-stricken moment she stared in confusion at the hand placed on her shoulder.

''I said, 'Excuse me. This is yours.' ''

The coldness in the voice almost made Alyson shiver as she quickly tried to regain composure and reach for the letter being extended to her. She wasn't prepared for the eyes that met hers. Dark, compelling eyes, seemingly filled with disdain as they glanced once again at the letter before turning to sweep over her. Alyson seized the paper, then self-consciously pushed back a tendril of her auburn hair, which had escaped from her French roll. Her light-green eyes flashed in anger as she realized this stranger was making no effort to disguise his disapproval of her.

Alyson mumbled a cursory, ''Thank you. It must have fallen from my lap,'' as she gathered up her documents and stuffed them into her briefcase.

His eyes focused on her as he replied smoothly, ''You're welcome, Miss Langdon. It *is* Miss Langdon, isn't it?''

The voice of the stewardess interrupted the embarrassing silence passing between them. Chad Braeburn flashed a tight, hard smile at her before returning to his seat to prepare for landing.

How dare he! Alyson felt indignant. What was it that had caused this stranger to react to her in such an odd manner?

And how did he know her name?

She quickly fastened her seat belt, taking care not to crush her silk blouse, and turned toward the window. The plane suddenly banked on approach to Whitehorse, sweeping alongside the mountain she would soon learn was Grey Mountain. Alyson's heart lurched as she caught sight of the majestic Yukon River, her thoughts a jumble of mixed emotions.

She suddenly felt out of place in this strange part of the country and unsure of her decision to come here. The vastness of the land itself was overwhelming, and it was apparent to her, after appraising the other passengers, that she was overdressed and clearly not one of the locals. And after her unsettling encounter, she wasn't sure she could be.

She glanced surreptitiously at the stranger who had so unnerved her. His looks were compelling. She took in his casual but obviously expensive attire and could recall the lingering smell of his leather jacket when his hand had rested on her shoulder. She would never forget the intensity of his almost-black eyes, in which were mirrored challenge. He was one of the most magnetic men she'd ever met.

Alyson chided herself for even thinking further about this stranger. He was intrusive and rude. He'd obviously read the letter before handing it back to her.

How else could he have connected the name to her? She only hoped that his manner wasn't indicative of the type of people she would meet. Best to forget about him . . . yet, why was he so abrupt?

She wasn't used to being in uncomfortable situations. Alyson was always the pacifier, always the compromiser, and was more than often referred to as "that sweet Alyson Langdon" by the residents of the nursing home where she worked. She took pride in knowing that her clients appreciated her good temper and patience. Her immediate reaction to this man's open disapproval of her had produced a flash of anger that had surprised her in its intensity.

The 737 gave a slight jolt as its wheels hit the runway; a short thrust completed its touchdown. *Almost there,* she thought as the plane taxied smoothly to the terminal. A two-hour stopover in Whitehorse, and then on to Dawson City and her final destination—her precious three-week vacation, to be spent sorting out what on earth she would do with this land she had so unexpectedly and so unwillingly inherited.

At least she'd have lots of tales to tell of Canada's North when she returned to her charges back in civilization. *That is, if I get back in one piece,* she mused as she reached for her hand luggage in the overhead rack. "Watch out for the grizzlies!" That's all Grampa Hill could say when she'd told them about her planned visit to the Yukon. "And the wolves. And the flies." Old Mrs. Parsons had insisted she should keep her delicate skin covered at all times; otherwise she'd be "eaten alive by all them black flies and mosquitoes." Her trip had kept the nursing home buzzing with speculation and stories for the last two weeks. Mrs. Parsons had even gotten carried away enough to marry her off to a rich gold miner. Alyson almost laughed out loud as she thought of the absurdity of the idea. She was well settled in San Francisco, thank you very much, and had no intention of becoming a pioneering amazon of the wild.

The short trek down the ramp brought Alyson into the terminal. She was pleasantly surprised by the modern look of the building: two carousels on her right already shooting out luggage in a rhythmic fashion, neat groupings of black leatherette chairs sectioned off into smoking and nonsmoking areas, large tropical plants and ferns set in cedar planters, native beadwork and artistry displayed in large, glassed-in cases.

"Welcome back, Mr. Braeburn. Your plane is waiting," came a voice from behind her.

"Thanks, Jake. Always good to get home."

Alyson didn't have to turn around to recognize the voice. The cold tone was missing, but it clearly belonged to the stranger who now possessed a name—Mr. Braeburn. She couldn't resist stealing a glance at the man who had so recently angered her—and attracted her.

Her eyes moved upward from the sleek cut of his boots to the tautness of the muscles visible under the tight-fitting jeans. The open shirt beneath his leather jacket revealed a thatch of black, curly hair. Around his neck he wore a chain with a large gold nugget the size of a pebble. It was a kind of pendant she had never seen before. She took in the features of his rugged, chiseled face, focusing finally on his full, sensual lips that suddenly twisted into a lopsided grin. Alyson froze as she realized the grin was aimed at her. The twinkle in his eyes conveyed the suggestion that he had observed her assessment of him and was amused by the embarrassment she now clearly showed. There was no mistaking the mischievous smile he gave before she had a chance to turn away.

"See you around, Cheechako," were the last words she heard as he and Jake swept past her and headed out of the terminal toward the runway.

"What's a Cheechako?"

Alyson tried to sound nonchalant as she picked up the thread of conversation again with the old gentleman seated next to her on the tiny, eight-passenger plane headed for Dawson City. It was obvious to her that he was a man of these parts, and she didn't want to appear ridiculously naive in her questioning. As it was, she had already attracted too much attention for her liking. Her green linen suit, champagne silk blouse, and matching pumps did much to accentuate her auburn hair and light-green eyes, but her ensemble was decidedly out of place here. T-shirts, jeans, and running shoes seemed to be the standard attire for male and female, young and old alike.

"A Cheechako? Well, let me see how to put that rightly." Her companion scratched thoughtfully at his beard before replying in a slow, deliberate tone, "A Cheechako ain't so bad, really. Some folks come here from Outside. They want to experience the wilderness, so they drive the Alaska Highway in their fancy recreational vehicles and think they've been a part of it all. They're Cheechakos. And then there's them that move here with their newfangled ideas all set to civilize the barbarians—until it gets cold. Then they hightail it back home with their tails between their legs. Can't wait to get back to someplace warm. They're Chee-chakos.''

"Oh." Alyson fell silent. She almost wished she hadn't asked.

Cheechako had been constantly ringing in her ears as she had reenacted the humiliating scene over and over in her mind. Each time she had tried to come up with some retort that would have put Mr. Braeburn firmly in his place; each time the scenario had left her at a loss for words.

Three hours had now passed, and Alyson could still feel her cheeks smarting with embarrassment at having been so openly exposed for actually staring at the man. She had been caught in the act, and no matter how she twisted and turned the events of those few moments, she knew that the stranger had physically attracted her and her admiration had shown all over her face. Alyson groaned inwardly. *This will be one encounter I defi-nitely will not be sharing with old Mrs. Parsons and her cronies when I get back,* Alyson vowed. She couldn't explain her own actions to herself; how on earth would she be able to explain to them why she had made such an utter fool of herself?

In fact, the whole day had not gone well. Despite all the care she had spent in packing for her trip, she'd had a vague sense of misgiving and inadequacy about the clothes she was taking. She'd had little time to find out about this place she had chosen to visit. The taxi driver on the way to the airport had, in his friendliness, added to her sense of unease.

"The Yukon? I've never heard of anybody going to the Yukon before. It's all muskeg, Eskimos, and igloos up there. You'd better have lots of warm clothes with you. You'll need them where you're going."

Alyson had managed to dispel her mood of doom and gloom a little on the flight from San Francisco to Vancouver. She remembered how her father had talked to her of brilliantly colored alpine flowers, water so clear you could see fish actually swimming by, tall green spruce trees, and air sweet with its freshness. He'd talked of one day going back to this place he had visited in his youth, the memory of which had never faded from his mind. Alyson hadn't realized how serious he had been in his desire to return until she'd been told by Mr. Asquith that he had actually bought some land there.

The stop in Vancouver had kindled once again a sense of misgiving. The waiting area of Gate 6 for Whitehorse had been full of people who all seemed to know each other. She alone had been left ungreeted, sitting apart from what seemed to be a strange communal group who knew at least someone there on a first-name basis. The plane ride to Whitehorse would have allowed her time to counterbalance any awkward feelings if she hadn't had that unfortunate encounter with Mr. Braeburn.

And now she was beginning to worry about where she was going to spend the night. It was already early evening, and the travel agent in San Francisco hadn't been able to book her into a hotel in Dawson City, as no hotels had been listed. Apparently it was just too unusual a place to merit keeping information on. However, she knew that Dawson City had been the capital city until 1951, when it had changed to Whitehorse. Whitehorse had been small but modern enough, judging by its airport. Dawson City was certain to be that much grander.

"Why doesn't the plane go directly from Vancouver to Dawson City?" she asked her companion on the plane.

"Well, most people get off in Whitehorse," he answered as if it were a question only a child would ask.

Alyson turned her attention to the land spread out below. The sun was catching the tips of the smaller mountains that glowed a mixture of pink and gold. The dark-green trees seemed to be endless, broken only by the meandering turquoise of rivers and lakes. Nowhere was there a sign of habitation—nothing.

"This land is never ending," she murmured, half aloud, half to herself.

"This is God's land, miss. People here live with the land; it's part of 'em. Otherwise they wouldn't stay."

"Yes, that's what my father used to tell me. He'd say some line out of a poem about, 'The farness that fills you with wonder, the stillness that fills you with peace.' "

"That's Robert Service. The Bard of the Yukon, he's called. You'll be hearing lots of Robert Service while you're here. Nearly everybody knows some line or other of his; his poetry grips you, if you know what I mean. The way he talks about this land makes you feel proud and strong. Because you have to be strong to survive here.''

The pride in his voice made Alyson look at him more closely; it had the same tone and reverence her father's voice had whenever he talked of the North, as though its land and people were of a distinct and noble line. It wasn't just the clothing that had set her apart on the plane from Vancouver and now from Whitehorse; it was something about belonging. Her mind flipped back to Mr. Braeburn's, ''See you around, Cheechako.'' There had been a certain amount of scorn in the way he had said it. She had felt it then, and she felt more convinced of it now.

It was certainly going to be a different vacation—that was for sure.

Alyson's jaw set. She was here to learn more of her father, make decisions about some property he had bought, and, if possible, enjoy herself. She wasn't going to be intimidated or made to feel weak simply because she was from the city. If the clothes she had chosen to wear today with so much care and excitement drew unacceptable attention to her—well, fine. She was who she was, and they could jolly well like it.

''There it is, miss. Off over there.''

''What? Where?'' Alyson replied, straining to spot some landmark amid the denseness of the trees.

''Dawson City. Top of the world, so to speak,'' came the response with a hint of mischief in the voice.

Alyson peered eagerly through the window. She

caught a glimpse of shining metal roofs and what appeared to be a handful of buildings that would fit into the palm of her hand.

"That's it?" she asked. "Just those few buildings by the river?"

"That's it. Don't look like much from here, does it? It was called the Little Paris of the North once. But it's a boom-and-bust town like all mining towns; Dawson's been bust for almost fifty years. It's burned down three times. Right to the ground twice. But it's still there for those of us who are survivors. Who're you visiting there, anyhow?"

Alyson was taken aback at the bluntness of the question. She wasn't visiting anyone — that was the trouble. She had decided to come in response to some instinctive call inside her that told her she had to see this land of her father's if she was ever to come to terms with him and ultimately his death. The sensations inside her were too fragile, however, to risk exposing to a stranger on an airplane.

"I'm not visiting anyone. I just want to visit the Yukon. It's been a dream . . . and this summer I had the chance to come, so here I am. Perhaps you know of a hotel where I could stay?" She shifted the conversation onto practical, safer ground.

"A hotel? Well, there's not many hotels to choose from. At this time of year it might be hard to find someplace. It's the tourist season, you know. Old Kate has some cabins for rent, though. They're not the Ritz, but they're clean and cozy, and old Kate will take good care of you. She loves telling folks like you yarns about old Dawson City. She's told so many stories for so long, even she doesn't remember what's true and what isn't. But if you've got half a mind to listen to her, she'll look after you like one of her own. Tell her Tom Hanson sent you, and she'll find a space for you somewhere.''

"That's very kind of you. Thank you.'' Alyson smiled gratefully at him.

"Don't forget to tell her Tom sent you. That's all. I'll point the way when we arrive. We should be there in five minutes.''

The plane hadn't come to a full stop, but all eight passengers were already on their feet and reaching for their bits and pieces of luggage. Tom stepped into the aisle to let Alyson pass in front of him as the plane finally stopped its bumping and the captain turned off the engines. This time the passengers stepped directly off the plane onto the runway.

The sweetness of the air almost made Alyson gasp. She stopped midway down the plane steps and took a deep breath.

"The air is so fresh.'' She turned to Tom. "I've never smelled air fresh like this.''

He, too, took a deep breath.

"That's right, miss. I told you. It's God's land.''

Despite the lateness of the hour, the day was still flooded in sunlight. Alyson checked her watch to confirm she hadn't made a mistake. It was certainly eleven o'clock, but the day was as bright as midafternoon. The warmth of the evening sun was a pleasant warmth. She was used to the muggy heat of a San Francisco summer that hit you like a soggy wave as soon as you ventured out. The freshness and the dryness of the warm air made her feel energetic and ready to go. It had been a long day of travel, but now she forgot the tiredness and her sense of unease.

She had finally arrived in her father's land.

Chapter Two

"Have some more muffins," Kate offered, clucking over Alyson like an old mother hen.

"They're delicious, Kate, but I couldn't. Thank you." Alyson smiled at her hostess. She felt wonderful. Kate had fussed over her as if she were a child, getting her settled into the cabin the night before, flicking at imaginary dust, and checking that she had all she needed for the night. The warmth of her welcome had immediately assuaged all the niggling doubts Alyson had been harboring about her visit.

"That Tom Hanson," she said. "He'll be the death of me. He finds all the waifs and strays out there and sends them over to old Kate. But somehow I always find room. I've been going to retire going on fifteen years, but old Tom just keeps 'em coming, and I just keep on enjoying them. My mother always used to say,

14

'The devil finds work for idle hands to do,' so I reckon I might as well keep on working.''

Her fussing and nattering reminded Alyson of her charges back home. It was good to feel back in familiar territory.

The cabin exuded the same warmth and openness as its mistress. The rough-hewn logs of the walls had grown smooth and shiny in places with age, and they glowed a rich, golden color in the sun's rays. Divided in two lengthwise, the simple rectangular building managed to provide a living room and eating area overlooking the dirt road and the river at the front of the building, and a bedroom and bathroom tucked discreetly behind. The furnishings were simple and unpretentious: a small kitchen table with two wooden chairs, two large overstuffed armchairs, an end table and lamp, an old potbellied stove in the corner, and a large double bed.

The cozy atmosphere was created by the gaily colored chintz curtains neatly tied with bows, the plump printed-cotton cushions, the handwoven scatter rugs, and the bunches of dried flowers in old earthenware pots. The crowning glory was the quilted bedspread made of a myriad of small scraps of fabric neatly stitched in the traditional log-cabin design. Alyson knew the hours that must have gone into the making of the quilt; she had watched old Mrs. Parsons and a number of her other charges painstakingly stitch away at patchwork squares they had been working on as long as she had been working at the home. It was true their fingers had seen better days, and they fumbled at their work now. Whoever had sewn this quilt had put a lot of time and patience in the work.

"It's beautiful." Alyson had fingered the bedspread reverently. Kate beamed.

It was well past midnight when Alyson climbed into bed that night, and it was a long time before sleep came. She was just too excited, too scared. Not scared in the true sense of the word, but the kind of "scared" she used to feel when she was on the brink of some sort of adventure—like when she sneaked off to the Hastings farm, cornered their palomino horse named Nicki, and rode her bareback across the field. Just the anticipation of it had made her shiver with excitement and, yes, fear. Fear at getting caught, fear at getting hurt. Still, the ten-year-old had done it, and she now remembered the power of exhilaration in that act of abandonment. It had been a good many years since she'd felt that way. The child was rarely evident in the woman she'd become. "Sweet, reliable, safe" Alyson Langdon had emerged somewhere along the way. Tonight Alyson the child had resurfaced. She had smiled at her thoughts.

Alyson didn't normally open up to strangers—or even acquaintances, for that matter. In San Francisco one didn't talk of one's feelings or business so readily. Kate, however, didn't feel like a stranger or an acquaintance.

Warm, witty, tough, down-to-earth Kate. In the span of an hour she'd listened to Alyson and regaled her with tales of the Klondike, tales that spanned a fifty-year period. She looked every bit her sixty-six years, and it suited her just fine. Her hair was still a rich black, even though traces of gray were visible. Her beauty, which must have been stunning years ago, was still evident, but most of it came from within.

Kate seemed to know everyone who lived, or had ever lived, in Dawson City. Alyson had recognized immediately that Kate was special and that she would remember her long after her return to San Francisco. San Francisco. It already seemed as if it were a lifetime away—a memory, Alyson realized, that held little fondness. This surprised her.

"I suppose, Kate, I'll have to find out exactly where this land is, then make arrangements to get out there," Alyson said as she finished her breakfast.

"Perhaps you should check first at the Mining Recorder's Office," Kate offered, "but, by the sound of it, I'd say it was out toward Hunker's Creek, about fifty miles southeast of town. Just check with Steve McClay at the Mining Recorder's Office. He'll set you straight from there, dear."

Kate's directions to the Mining Recorder's Office were easy to follow. Alyson walked along the dirt road by the river and took the first turn to the left. There was Main Street. It was hard to miss. It was the only street she had come across with stores and commercial buildings. Other streets en route had been less than a city block in length. The homes she had seen didn't resemble those in San Francisco's city streets. There was a higgledy-piggledy mixture of shiny new log homes, dilapidated clapboard cottages, and mobile homes in random order. What struck Alyson most was the enormous size of the vegetables growing in the yards. The rhubarb was almost taller than she was, and the cabbages looked like giant footballs. *It must be all the sunshine they get in summer,* she thought. *Unless there's something more than gold in the soil here.* She made a note to remind herself to ask Kate when she got back to the cabin.

The streets were almost devoid of people. A few with cameras around their necks passed by—obviously tourists. The size of the vegetation must also have struck them as unusual, for she saw more than one person posing for a picture with a giant cabbage as background. The locals were easy to spot—they were the ones driving by in trucks of all shapes and sizes, with at least one large dog in the back. She spotted a few Labradors and mongrels, but the majority by far were huskies.

They suit this place, Alyson mused. Solid and independent, almost proud of being uncivilized. They didn't come running up to you for a pat and attention like the well-fed, pampered pets she was used to seeing. They had their own territory, which they guarded noisily as soon as anyone got too close to the truck that signified their domain. Neither were they unfriendly; they simply didn't need attention or acceptance from humans.

Alyson was consciously taking mental note of all the odd thoughts that passed through her mind as she headed for the office on Main Street. She would probably never visit this place again after she had sold her father's property, but she wanted to collect details to remember and think about later. First, however, she had to go and see the property for herself. It obviously had meant a great deal to her father, and to sell it from San Francisco without even setting foot on it had seemed too callous an act.

As she entered the door of the Office of the Mining Recorder, Chad Braeburn stepped out of the doorway opposite. The sign overhead identified the legal firm of Dalton & Dalton. He had caught sight of Alyson moments before as she headed toward him down Main Street and had quickly stepped back into the lawyers' office before she had had a chance to spot him. It would have been very awkward if she had come to arrange an appointment with Jim Dalton right then. He'd just finished talking to him about his company's offer to purchase Harry Langdon's land and had been told that nothing had been received from Mr. Langdon since his refusal to sell the land four months ago.

Darn that girl; what was she doing here? She was presumably Langdon's daughter, not his wife, since Chad had seen no wedding band on her hand, and she had admitted to the name Langdon on the plane when he handed her back the letter from his lawyers to her father. Chad frowned. What on earth was she doing here? The price he'd offered on the land was triple the amount Langdon had paid for it. His lips hardened into a thin, straight line. He needed that land badly and was willing to pay for it. But he wasn't willing to be taken for a ride by someone who had no real interest in this place and was just out to milk him for all he had.

"Did you forget something, Mr. Braeburn?" The receptionist smiled hopefully at him.

"No, Sally. I thought I did, but I guess I didn't," Chad fumbled. He'd known Sally for years; he also knew what that hopeful expression on her face meant, and he felt guilty. Sally was an attractive young woman, but he didn't want to start a relationship he knew she would be more than willing to encourage. Romances could turn into nasty situations in a small town, and Chad had no desire to end up having his own lawyer as his enemy. He saw Alyson go into the building opposite.

"Look after yourself, Sally. I'll be in contact with Jim later this week."

Before Sally had a chance to reply, Chad was out of the door. *Such a handsome man. What a waste!* she sighed to herself. Chad Braeburn was almost a legend among her contemporaries. He was one of the few eligible bachelors around, and he seemed to have it all—good looks, money, charm. But neither she nor her friends seemed to hold any attraction for him. He was always polite and courteous and made a point of dancing with anyone who was left out at any of the local dances, but he always came alone and left alone. Someday somebody was going to break through that barrier of his, she thought, and he wouldn't know what hit him. *But it's not going to be you, Sally, my girl,* she told herself, *so you might as well face it.*

Chad stared moodily at the Office of the Mining Recorder. *So, Miss Langdon certainly isn't losing any time,* he thought grimly to himself. *But why on earth has she turned up out of the blue like this?*

The letter he had picked up on the plane had hit him like a thunderbolt. He had been admiring the woman in the aisle across from him for most of the trip. There was no one thing he could identify about her that accounted for her attraction. In fact, there was almost an air of sadness as she intently read and reread the papers she was holding. Perhaps it was the way she kept closing her eyes, as though to hold back tears and gather strength, that made her look so vulnerable. And he had felt a sudden strong urge to reach out and put his arms around her. It was a feeling he thought he had discarded long ago.

For years he had immersed himself in work and eventually found solace and protection in it. There had been times, he must confess, when he felt lonely and wondered what on earth he was going to do with all his success when he had no one to share it with him. But it was a choice he had made, and he was glad of it.

When one piece of paper slipped from her lap and floated across the aisle to land near his feet, he had picked it up eagerly, glad to have an opportunity to talk to her. The familiar crest on the letterhead had caught his attention immediately, and one quick glance at the salutation told him exactly why this young woman was on the plane. The realization that she must be on the way to Dawson City to see his lawyer about the Langdon property dispelled immediately all feelings of tenderness, and suspicion and caution took their place.

Now Chad deliberated what his next move should be. His firm needed the Langdon property badly, but he couldn't very well accost her in the middle of the street and demand to know what she was up to. He needed to tread carefully here. Dawson City was a small town; he would find out about her easily enough.

Shrugging, he headed for Joe's Café. Many of his workers who were in town would be there, and it was a point of honor with him that he never lose contact with the grass roots of his organization. His father had built Klondike Enterprises and had never forgotten what it was like to work in the mines. He'd been a miner for twenty years before taking the plunge and setting out on his own with a modest prospector's claim. Without the help of money borrowed from his mining pals, he would never have been able to work the claim on Hunker's Creek.

Chad couldn't remember when his father made his fortune; he had been well-off as long as he could remember, and Chad had been sent to private boarding schools and university to study engineering with the best that money could buy. He had taken over from his father in his early twenties. As the boss's son, he had encountered the resentment often harbored by employees for his like. It had taken months of dedicated effort, working in the mine alongside the men, to gain the respect accorded his father. He was comfortable with them now and proud that his company had never felt the need to become unionized.

Coffee would be just the right thing to clear his head.

Alyson folded the piece of paper containing directions to Hunker's Creek and tucked it securely in her shoulder bag. Kate had been right about the location, fifty miles southeast of Dawson. All she needed now was transportation. With this in mind, she set off once more up Main Street, calculating half an hour to locate a garage and arrange a car rental. She should be able to make the fifty-mile trip in less than an hour; that would allow her time for a quick look around today before heading back to Kate's. Then she could take stock and plan the best use of her time for the next three weeks. So far the day had gone well. Alyson smiled to herself. Yesterday she had allowed herself to get rattled and nervous; today she was filled with her usual sense of optimism and confidence.

Gold Nugget Saloon, The Last Frontier, Bonanza, the Eldorado—she savored the names of the cafés and stores as she passed by. Everything was so different.

A magnificent display of gold-nugget jewelry caught her eye, and despite the organizing of her time a moment ago, she couldn't resist the temptation to stop and peer through the store window. The nuggets of pure gold were fashioned into rings, earrings, watchbands, bracelets, brooches, and necklaces—all distinguished from each other by the size and shape of the nugget. It was the rawness she liked, as though each piece were saying, "I will not be changed and prettied up. I am what I am." That's what she'd like to take back as her souvenir, she resolved.

She stared intently at the rings, looking from one to the other, weighing this one against that one. Suddenly the gleam of a large gold nugget on a chain, much larger than the ones displayed, was reflected in the windowpane. Someone was obviously standing beside her, but she had been so intent in her inspection, she hadn't heard the approach.

"They have their own special beauty, don't they?" The sound of the voice set Alyson's heart racing. It couldn't be—not here of all places. She took a deep breath to steady herself and turned to respond to the owner of the voice. The name Braeburn had flashed instantly through her mind as soon as the words were said, but she was still unprepared for the shock she felt as she turned and saw that he really was standing next to her.

"I didn't mean to startle you, Miss Langdon. I'm sorry." An amused look crossed his face. "It was an innocent remark, I assure you."

Alyson could feel the blood rushing to her face. For the second time in as many days she had been taken completely by surprise by this man. She searched desperately for some remark to make, but before she could catch one of the thoughts jumbled in her head, she heard the smooth voice continue, "If I hadn't met you yesterday, I would have taken you for a university student visiting a friend on vacation. Jeans and a ponytail—who would believe it?"

The lopsided grin and laughing eyes sent her back to the scene in the airport, but she was determined to take her leave of this meeting with dignity. "How nice to see you again, Mr. Braeburn." Her tone belied her words.

"I'm flattered you took the time to find out my name. I wonder why you went to so much trouble. However, if you're to be staying in Dawson for a while, I'm sure we will be running into each other again, and Mr. Braeburn sounds a little too formal for this part of the country, don't you agree? The name's Chad."

Alyson shook his extended hand, thankful he hadn't pursued the question of where she had learned his name. Eavesdropping on other people's conversations at airports was hardly dignified behavior.

"Alyson," she said simply.

"I see our gold has taken your fancy. You'd better be careful. You may end up with gold fever. It's an infectious disease here. Of course, you're probably here to study turn-of-the century architecture or the effect of wilderness living on isolated communities."

The hint of sarcasm irked Alyson. *Cheechako,* she thought. *That's what he's thinking. Someone from Outside who's come here to go home afterward and boast about braving the formidable wilderness.*

"Actually, Mr. Braeburn, I'm here on business." Alyson deliberately refrained from calling him Chad. "I need to get out to my property on Hunker's Creek, and if you would kindly tell me where I can rent a car, I'll be—"

Chad's burst of laughter left her sentence unfinished. Alyson stared at him in disbelief. He had thrown back his head and was laughing uncontrollably. It was a rich laugh that didn't have any malice in it, but Alyson couldn't think of anything she had said that was so uproariously funny.

"Rent a car!" Chad managed to get out. "Rent a car!" He wiped at his eyes. "Alyson, this is Dawson City. Nobody rents a car in Dawson. There aren't even taxis in this place. And Hunker's Creek is off a dirt road. I doubt anyone would get over the rough road with a car still intact. However," he continued, putting a sober expression on his face, "I would be delighted to come to your rescue. It just so happens I'm going that way today. I could drop you off on the way. . . ."

"Thank you, Mr. Braeburn. I'm perfectly capable of finding some way of getting out there on my own. Good day." Alyson turned her back on him and walked away. She looked straight ahead. How could she have been so naive? What a stupid, dim-witted person he must think she was!

"I'll be leaving at two o'clock. If you change your mind, you'll be able to find me at the Eldorado."

Alyson heard the words plainly but didn't acknowledge them or slow her steps. She turned left at the first corner she came to and once out of sight leaned against the wall of the building.

Her knees felt as though they would crumble under her as she slumped against the building wall. Anger welled up in her. Just who did this man think he was, making comments on her dress, putting himself on a first-name basis, laughing at a foolish but perfectly understandable mistake about car rentals, and then having the nerve to offer to take her out to Hunker's Creek himself? She took a deep breath. *Get a hold of yourself, Alyson, for heaven's sake. Chad Braeburn is just someone who has nothing better to do than read other people's letters and stick his nose into other people's affairs.* Kate would probably know someone who had a spare truck or whatever that she could rent. Chad Braeburn could just go find some other Cheechako to tease.

Alyson made no mention of her meeting with Chad Braeburn to Kate. She was on edge, nervous about conducting an important business transaction that she knew virtually nothing about. The news that the property wasn't easy to get to had thrown an unexpected kink in her plans. Yesterday it had been relatively clear in her mind: Find a place to stay, go look at the property, arrange to see the lawyers who had been communicating with her father, make arrangements for the sale, then enjoy the rest of the time sight-seeing. Now Chad Braeburn had managed to put her in a flap about finding transportation. It was irrational, she knew, to focus her frustration on him. She merely asked Kate if she knew of anyone who would be willing to drive her out for one quick look or lend her a truck for a few hours.

"There's no need to look as though the end of the world has come," Kate consoled. "There are lots of miners in Klondike Enterprises, and there's bound to be a few of them in town who'll be heading out that way. I'm sure I can arrange for someone to get you there and back today. I'll phone right now and see what I can do."

Alyson could hear Kate's voice from the next room. She couldn't hear the exact words, but she caught odd drifts . . . "A nice young lady from San Francisco . . . her property . . . oh, she'll be ever so pleased . . . Cabin 3 . . . I'll tell her. . . ."

"Well, that's done," Kate crowed, bustling back into the kitchen. "People here are always glad to lend a hand. If you just want to grab a bite to eat before you go, you'll get picked up at a quarter to two or thereabouts. If you want, we could make some sandwiches and drinks for you to take. There won't be anything out there for you to buy, and it'll be late before you're back. And make sure you take a jacket with you. It can get cool in the evenings."

Alyson smiled at her. "Usually I'm the one reminding people to put on sweaters and make sure they have enough to eat. You make me feel like a kid again, Kate. I'm so glad I sat next to Tom on the plane. A hotel would have been nothing compared with this."

"Go on with you," Kate blustered. "All you had to do was smile, and you'd have had all of Dawson offering to take you out there. You just need to find your way around a bit, that's all. Now come on, we don't have much time."

Alyson was just reaching for her jacket when she heard someone knocking on the cabin door. "Coming," she called. Sandwiches and drinks ("Better take enough for two," Kate had said), camera, money for the ride, a jacket—yes, she had everything. She opened the door, a profusion of thanks already pouring out. She stopped midsentence.

"Kate said a lovely lady in Cabin 3 was in need of a ride," Chad said, grinning.

Chapter Three

Speechless, Alyson stood in the doorway. An eternity seemed to pass before she found her voice. All the while Chad leaned casually against the doorway.

"I . . . don't . . . believe you!" She finally responded with shocked disbelief. "You have the nerve to come here and—"

"Oh, there you are, Chad!" Kate shouted as she walked up the path. "You two have obviously made your introductions. Told you she was a sweet thing!"

Chad quirked an eyebrow as he turned to Alyson, replying, "You were always one to tell the truth, Kate. And I, of course, am always one to come to the rescue of someone in distress. Are you ready to go, Miss Langdon?" he asked solicitously.

Well! Alyson thought. *You aren't about to get out of this one. At least not without hurting Kate's feelings.*

*And I wouldn't do that for all the world, especially not
for the likes of Chad Braeburn.*

She brushed by Chad and called to Kate over her
shoulder, "See you later, and thanks for everything,
Kate."

Alyson sensed, rather than saw, Chad looking at her
from time to time as they drove along, but she kept
her eyes firmly on the road ahead. Suddenly he pulled
the truck over to the side of the road and stopped.

"This isn't going to work, Cheechako. We have got
a two-hour drive ahead of us in some of the most
beautiful country on this earth, and you're sitting there
putting out vibes that would make a man of a more
sensitive nature curl up and die. What do you say we
call a truce for the day?"

"What do you mean by a truce, Mr. Braeburn?"
Alyson said, turning to look him full in the face.

"I promise to behave like a true gentleman of the
South." Chad smiled back at her. "I hereby declare
that as of this moment I shall make no personal remarks
about your beauty, tempting though that is, and I shall
answer all questions with due respect and decorum. Is
it a deal?"

"And you'll refrain from calling me Cheechako?"
Alyson countered.

"If you will, in turn, refrain from calling me Mr.
Braeburn."

She turned to look at him. Her annoyance melted.
Gone was the grin; in its place, a disarming smile. This
man was positively unnerving. Okay, she decided, but
she didn't trust him. Or was it herself she didn't trust?

she wondered. That is, did she trust herself not to act like an inexperienced fool in front of him?

"Come now, Alyson, it's not that hard a decision to make, is it?" Chad spoke again, this time in a smooth, persuasive tone.

She could see the corners of his lips beginning to lift into that lopsided grin, a grin that he was seriously trying to keep under control. She looked away to hide the beginning of her own smile. He was right. It was a glorious day, and she wanted to enjoy the scenery. Her own emotions were getting in the way. Besides, there were a million questions she wanted to ask him.

"It's worth a try, I think," she finally replied. Her smile was genuine. "How do you do? My name is Alyson Langdon."

Chad grasped the extended hand firmly. "I'm delighted to make your acquaintance, Alyson. Welcome to the Yukon." The lopsided grin was no longer disguised, and his eyes lit up with a warmth that made her feel the sincerity behind the words.

"Well, let's get this truck on the road again, shall we?" Gently he released his hold on her hand and pulled back onto the road.

"Why did you say we had a two-hour trip ahead of us? Isn't Hunker's Creek only fifty miles from Dawson?" she asked.

"Ah, my dear Chee . . . Alyson," Chad corrected himself promptly, "dirt roads are not like the roads you're used to. If I were to travel along here at sixty miles an hour, we'd be in the ditch before you know it. But it's a varied ride. Half the time we spend avoiding potholes in the road; the other half we maneuver around boulders that have come down with the latest rainfall. You have the enviable position of sitting on the passenger side and will have full view of the five-hundred-foot drop-offs that appear along the way. The Alaska Highway has succumbed to guardrails to protect our esteemed tourists from hurtling to their deaths over the side; we, however, are the last of the pioneers and disdain such extravagant gentility.''

Alyson laughed. She liked his dry sense of humor now that she was no longer on the receiving end of it.

''Underestimating is a common mistake made by people who are new to the Yukon,'' Chad continued. ''Its vastness is hard to imagine, and so many places are not accessible by normal travel. Roads are few and far between, and those that do exist are very hard to maintain. Most of us brave the wilderness in four-wheel drives, as you can tell from mine. Even then, some-times the roads are in dismal condition. You'll enjoy the ride, though, I'm sure. The raw beauty of it will take your breath away.''

Chad's voice dropped to a mere whisper at the men-tion of the beauty of it. It held the same reverence that Tom Hanson's had held. She could almost feel it.

''You really love this country, don't you?''

''I was born and raised here. It's in my blood,'' he replied quickly. He paused for a moment and then continued. ''No, it's in my soul. I tried city living for a while. Just like most of the kids who grow up here, I couldn't wait to leave the place. Go somewhere with lots of action and lots of people. See the world. It took two years for me to get that out of my system. And then I couldn't wait to get rid of all that frantic bustling and activity and all those people. Everybody in such a hurry to get somewhere, desperately scrabbling through mounds of traffic and people to find someplace to escape. I've found the place where I'm at peace, and I wouldn't trade it for all the gold in the Yukon.''

I envy you, Alyson thought, studying the expression on Chad's face as he spoke. The conviction behind his words was evident: a mixture of tenderness and pride showed in his voice and his smile. For a brief moment, though, his eyes clouded, and she sensed an acknowledgment of something lacking, an element of sadness.

''Does your wife love this land as much as you do?'' The words were out of Alyson's mouth before she realized what she had said. The unexpectedness of the question shocked her, and a stunned silence hung between them before Chad replied.

''My wife loved city life. She couldn't find happiness here.'' The tone of his voice changed abruptly to one tinged with anger and regret. His lips hardened into a thin line, and Alyson saw the knuckles on his hand go white as he tightened his grip on the steering wheel.

She knew she had said the wrong thing and was angry with herself for asking a question that pried into his personal life. She floundered in her mind for a different topic, something to restore the mood of a moment ago, but all she could focus on were the words ''loved'' and ''couldn't.'' Where was his wife now?

''Apart from spending a few years Outside, I've been here for thirty-six years,'' Chad continued after a few moments.

Yes, Alyson thought, thankful to him for returning

the conversation to safer ground. *I guessed him to be in his thirties.* His face didn't show age as much as it showed "living." Rugged but unlined, except for a few laugh lines around his mouth. Probably from that aggravating grin that surfaced when he was amused. She'd had occasion to see that in her few humiliating encounters with him over the past two days.

"Kate said that there's a mining company near Hunker's Creek," Alyson finally managed to say, "and that I'd probably be able to get a ride with one of the miners from there. Is that where you work?"

"Yes, that's where I work. It's a gold mine, in the figurative as well as the literal sense of the word. It's hard work, but I have no complaints. But tell me about you. What exactly are you doing here? Thinking of going into prospecting?" The corners of Chad's lips framed a gently mocking smile, but the eyes peered keenly into Alyson's as he waited for her reply.

She shrugged off the question. "I might if I thought I'd make my fortune," she replied flippantly. "I'm just looking at my options right now."

"I see."

She had no idea what options she might be looking at. The thought of developing the land had never occurred to her, nor did she have any intentions beyond seeing the place and selling it. However, she felt a strange need to prove herself in some way to this man, and somehow, considering business options seemed like an impressive idea. Further discussion of non-existent proposals would, she knew, get her flustered and hesitant. Dissembling wasn't one of her strong points. Once again she found herself floundering. Both of them lapsed into silence.

Alyson was beginning to regret that she had even attempted to impress this man with her flippancy. He didn't strike her as being the kind who impressed easily. It was totally out of character for her to be anything other than candid in her responses. Men in general didn't intimidate her, at least none she'd met so far. But this one was entirely different. In the short time she'd known him, he'd managed to draw out reactions she didn't even recognize, let alone understand. And now he just sat there with his black eyes veiled in . . . distrust? Disappointment?

The truck came to a stop, jolting her from her thoughts. Now what? Another heart-to-heart?

"Really, Alyson, you should delay considering your business options." Chad turned to her and smiled. "You're missing an opportunity to witness the wonders of this place." His voice lowered to a conspiratorial whisper. "Look over there to your right."

Clambering over a stump were two black bear cubs. Alyson's smile lit up her eyes. "They're adorable!" she cried. "And to see them like this in their natural environment—wonderful!" She turned and beamed at Chad. He was clearly pleased with her excitement.

She put her hand on the car door.

"No!" Chad's voice cut in sharply, and he reached across and grabbed her hand. "Never, never get out of a vehicle to take a look outside; no matter how cute those cubs look, there's—"

Alyson turned to him in fury.

"Let go of my hand! Just how stupid do you think I am? I was going to wind up the window. In case you hadn't noticed, it's rolled halfway down, and I have no intention of leaving it that way in case the mother bear comes along and sees me as a potential threat to her young ones and decides to defend them by making mincemeat out of me. So if you don't mind. . . ."

He released his hold on her hand. With the window firmly rewound, she turned back to him, her eyes flashing.

"What is it with you?" she demanded. "For five minutes we manage to carry on a reasonably sane conversation; then just when everything seems to be going okay, I manage to say or do something that you find ridiculously absurd. You point out every mistake I make because I'm not familiar with the territory, as though I've committed the greatest sin on earth, and then you have the audacity to think I'd be naive enough to get out and play with a couple of wild animals like some kittens in a barnyard."

Tears of rage filled her eyes. She could hear the near hysteria in her voice as she spat the words at him. "Oh, what's the point?" she said numbly. She looked back toward the cubs.

"Alyson."

She continued to stare resolutely out of the window. She couldn't trust herself to speak.

"Alyson, I'm so sorry. I don't think you're stupid. It's just that I thought you were going to get out and. . . ." Chad's voice trailed off, and he left the sentence unfinished.

She turned to look at him. He was obviously embarrassed.

He took a deep breath and looked her squarely in the face. "I said I'm sorry, and I mean it. I apologize for insulting you by suggesting—or even thinking—that you didn't know any better than to invite danger." There was no disputing the genuineness in his voice, and his eyes reflected a respect that hadn't been there before.

Alyson could feel the anger of the previous moment melting away. For one fleeting second she had the irresistible urge to put her arms around the contrite figure next to her. The feeling was so intense, she had to look away.

"Please, Alyson," he continued. "I'm truly sorry."

"It's okay. Really," she managed to mumble. "Let's forget it. I just wish we could enjoy watching the cubs play. It's not every day a city slicker like me gets a firsthand experience like this," she added mischievously.

Chad grinned back in relief.

"See how they treat that stump, as if it were a toy made especially for their enjoyment." He once again diverted her attention to the cubs, which were awkwardly climbing up one side of the stump of an uprooted tree, then rolling uncontrollably down the other side. He leaned closer to her and rested his hand casually behind her shoulders. "I'm sure they're laughing," he whispered intimately.

Alyson was startled by the warmth of his breath on her neck, and although her face was still burning from the exchange of a moment ago, she flushed even more at the sensation of closeness. To turn to look at him would cause her further humiliation. He would clearly be able to see the effect he was having on her. She simply leaned forward as if trying to get a closer look at the cubs, in an attempt to gain control of her emotions.

"Isn't it true that black bears are normally not dangerous unless there's an implied threat toward their cubs?" she asked. "I mean, out here, they really aren't a menace, are they?" She continued looking out the window as she spoke.

"That's true. It's not black bears that concern us, at least not if we use common sense. Their behavior is fairly predictable. Now, take grizzlies. That's a different matter." Chad leaned back in his seat, removing his arm from behind her shoulders.

"Have you had problems with grizzlies out at Hunker's Creek?" Alyson was never troubled by the dangers of the wild back in San Francisco—not of the animal kind, that is. She sensed that she was in for a firsthand account of one of those spine-tingling, real-life stories that she had only read about. She rationalized that she was really only interested in being able to recount adventurous tales to her charges at the nursing home, simply because she knew they would enjoy them immensely.

"Well, have you?" She gently prodded him to continue.

"People have encountered problems with grizzlies all over the Yukon. Some attacks have taken place as close as fifteen miles from major centers. Hunker's Creek is fifty miles from Dawson City, so naturally we come across grizzlies as a matter of course. Maulings—and deaths—have been dealt by grizzlies, but there's one particular incident that sends shivers down my spine when I think of it.''

Alyson grew still as she turned her full attention to him. His face showed little expression as he gazed toward the cubs, who were still enjoying their frolic.

"Two years ago friends of mine, Bob and Lee Edmonds, lived in a two-story log house Bob built not far from Hunker's Creek," Chad began his tale. "They lived there with their two sons, Barry and young Bobby. During the day Bob worked at the mine. Lee was being harassed by a grizzly that seemed to come around in the daytime—never at night, for some reason. At first she ignored it, since it didn't do anything except prowl around the vicinity. She just went inside with the boys until it left. Gradually, though, the bear became more of a threat—standing to look in the windows, banging up against the door.''

Alyson could feel her heart flutter as she imagined the scene.

Chad's voice lowered as he continued, ''One day Lee became really frightened when the bear actually broke a window in the living room in an attempt to get in. She ran to the second floor with the boys and made an effort to barricade the stairs. Young Bob, who was twelve, wanted to get his gun and shoot the grizzly, but Lee thought he was still too young to be handling weapons outside the presence of his dad and felt safe enough upstairs. The bear finally left, but that night when Lee recounted the story to Bob, he decided it was high time he did something about it.'' Chad stopped for a moment.

''You see, Alyson, we have a respect for our animal inhabitants—they have more of a right to this territory than we do. We don't kill anything for the mere sake of doing so. But in this case the bear was obviously a danger to Bob's family. He decided he had to shoot it.''

''I understand,'' Alyson acknowledged.

''Bob felt certain the grizzly would return the next day and stayed home to confront him. The grizzly did come back, and Bob shot him. But he didn't kill him; he just wounded him. There is only one thing worse than an angry grizzly—a wounded, angry grizzly. Bob knew he would have to track him and finish the job. He took Bobby with him.''

This time Chad turned to Alyson and stared directly into her eyes as he continued his tale. Shivers overtook her body. From the story or from his gaze? she wondered.

''Bob and his son tracked the grizzly for two hours, following the trail of blood left by the wound. Bob crouched down, confused, to examine the trail; young Bobby was off to his right, rifle at the ready. Suddenly, behind him, came the unmistakable grunt of an enraged grizzly. Bob hadn't been tracking the grizzly; the grizzly had been tracking him!''

Alyson froze at the thought of it.

''Bob whirled around but didn't even have time to respond. In a flash he could see the seven hundred-pound animal lurching toward him; at the same time he heard an explosion he thought came from inside his head. The grizzly crashed two feet from him. In shock, he turned to see his twelve-year-old son lowering his rifle. He was overcome by uncontrollable shaking— and still is whenever he recounts the story. Bob says that the grizzly was operating on sheer rage, since there was barely a drop of blood left in him.''

Alyson was speechless and couldn't turn her eyes away from Chad's. They seemed locked in place.

''Don't underestimate a grizzly, Alyson. Intelligence combined with ferociousness make for a formidable enemy.''

More than anything, Alyson wanted to lean closer to him for protection and comfort. She was greatly affected by the story.

Chad shifted the truck back into gear and slowly started off again down the road.

''So how come such a city slicker knows so much about bears?'' he asked.

''I enjoy reading about nature, animal or human. And bear attacks make great headlines, even in a San Francisco paper. 'Man Mauled by Bear While on Vacation' gets lots of people reading, I assure you. Anyway, I am on strict orders from Grampa Hill to watch out for the grizzlies.''

''Your grandfather warned you?''

''No,'' Alyson laughed. ''Grampa Hill is one of the people at the home where I work. I'm supposed to be the one in charge, looking after his needs, but he spends most of his time giving me fatherly advice and telling me gruesome horror stories that would keep any self-respecting young lady securely locked away for safe-keeping.''

"You work in a home? I assumed you were a high-tech, new-age businesswoman," Chad said in a surprised tone. "You did say you were here on business. Your father obviously trusts you with his business matters."

"How do you know I'm here on my father's business? I never said that to you. Just how much of my father's letter did you read?"

Chad groaned. There was no mistaking the suppressed anger in Alyson's voice, and he couldn't blame her. The idea of telling Alyson that he was in fact the owner of Klondike Enterprises and that the letter had been written by his lawyer to her father at his instruction crossed his mind. But could he trust her? Why was she here in person? And why had there been no response to his more-than-generous offer to purchase the land? It was too risky at this early stage to give up the advantage he had. Sad, though, he reflected. He would have liked to have been honest with her. Better to let her think he had actually had the nerve to read a letter he had no business reading.

"I saw the letter was addressed to a Mr. Langdon. The name Klondike Enterprises caught my attention, and I recognized the letterhead as belonging to one of the firms in town. I just guessed at the rest."

"I must remember you have eyes like a hawk. I'll take care not to leave any papers lying around during my stay," she said icily.

The mention of her father had set her on edge. It had been a relief to talk to Kate, but her instinct warned her that this man wasn't quite to be trusted. Something about him disturbed her. Something that loomed up from nowhere just when everything seemed to be going well. Well, let him think her father had sent her to do his business. *I'm certainly not going to pour my heart out to this guy,* she resolved. *He thinks I'm crazy as it is, coming here to settle business. What on earth would he think if he knew I came here in search of a father I never really knew for a reason I don't even understand myself?*

Neither spoke for the next few miles. The silence, however, wasn't uncomfortable. Chad concentrated on slowing down for holes that opened up without warning in the middle of the road; Alyson took in the view of the ever-present mountains and scanned the roadside for more signs of wildlife.

"I see what you mean," she said as they turned a corner and she looked down at the sheer drop two feet from the edge of the road. "About the sharp drop, I mean. I wonder how many people have ended up in those gulleys."

"A few Cheechakos, no doubt," Chad said and grinned. "But somebody usually comes along just in time to rescue them. Actually, there are very few accidents. People seem to act in a saner way when it's obvious they'll lose unless they do. And Mother Nature is far too formidable an opponent in this part of the country to mess around with. You very rarely get a second chance. Occasionally someone lives to tell a tale, but not too often."

Alyson shuddered. "Are there really wolves that howl at night like some sepulchral ghost?"

"Oh, there are lots of wolves. You'll probably see one around while you're here. But wolves aren't much of a threat. The idea of a pack of wolves carrying off children in the middle of winter is just a fanciful myth. I don't think I've heard of a wolf attacking a human in all the time I've lived here. They're afraid of man and want nothing to do with him. There have been times that measures have been taken to control wolves coming into communities in search of food because nature's supply is too low for them to survive. Then cats and dogs become very tempting fare, and there just might be the risk that a child might be mistaken for fodder.

"If there are reports of wolves running in packs close to settlements, the government has to take some kind of protective action. Unfortunately, poison is one of the solutions. At this time of the year, though, there's lots for everyone to eat. So you needn't worry on that score. And the wolf howl is an eerie sound only if nature frightens you. I like the sound. It reminds me of the rights of all forms of life."

Alyson smiled to herself. What a strange mixture this man was! And the thought suddenly struck her that within the space of forty-eight hours she had seen many sides of this man's character and spent many hours thinking of him.

She lapsed into silence as she reflected on her past relationships.

Her infatuation with Luke had lasted almost two years; she had thought herself deeply in love with him at the time and had never really managed to explain to herself why she had broken off the relationship. The idea of a permanent commitment like marriage had frightened her, while at the same time the idea of a future without marriage had seemed pointless. That was five years ago. How grown up and mature she had thought herself then—with a stable job, an apartment of her own, freedom at last from her mother's prying and interference.

Five years later, at twenty-seven, she lacked the sureness that she had once taken for granted. The decision to get in touch with her father, whom she had seen for one or two weeks a year during summer holidays as a kid and whom she'd later let drift away once she'd left home, came too late. By the time she managed to meet him in an attempt to pick up the threads of their lives and get to understand him, he was suffering from cancer. His death came a mere six months later. The suddenness of it all had left an emptiness and confusion that had shaken her confidence in herself. Chad was the first person to have occupied her thoughts so intensely for a long time.

"A penny for your thoughts," Chad said, glancing at her briefly.

"I was just wondering how much farther," she said quietly. She ignored the eyebrows raised in an expression of polite disbelief.

"Too bad. I thought you were preparing for a great debate on equal rights for man and wolf. I was looking forward to some intellectual rebuttal. But I see you aren't quite in the mood for wit and repartee."

Alyson was glad he had lapsed back into the gentle teasing.

"Do you always set such high goals for your passengers? Or does a visitor from the great metropolis offer some kind of special challenge for you?'' she parried.

His laugh was rich and full. The wide, open mouth displayed a set of even white teeth, the eyes lost the veil that clouded over them in serious moments, and the tautness in his face disappeared as the muscles relaxed. The effect was one of open abandonment. *He's so attractive!* Alyson thought.

''You're so attractive!'' Hearing the words said out loud jolted Alyson. ''I mean,'' Chad continued, ''it's refreshing to find someone who can meet me on my own terms.''

''Perhaps your terms can go too far. The line between insult and compliment is easy to cross. A fool plays to win at all costs; a wise man knows when to stop.''

He smiled at her.

''How much farther is it, really?'' she asked.

''See those buildings over there?'' Chad pointed to the right. ''That's the camp for the men who work in the mine. Some men live in town, but many live in the camp itself. The Langdon property is adjacent to the mine. You'll see the cabin on it when we go over the next hill.''

''Cabin? I didn't know there was a cabin on the land.''

He gave her a quick, puzzled look. Nothing on Alyson's face portrayed deception. If she was playing coy, feigning surprise to increase the value of the property, she was doing a very good job. He had watched the building of the cabin carefully for the last three years. Each summer a little more had been added. At first he had felt a mild sense of curiosity. He'd been tempted to go over and introduce himself to the man who turned up each July, but summer had been the busiest time of the year for him.

By the time pressure at work had eased, the man had disappeared. This year, however, Chad had a strong interest in what was going on, and busy or not he had determined to talk to him, to persuade him to sell. He was surprised Alyson didn't know of the building her father had done. A lot of time and money had been invested in the project.

The cabin came into sight as soon as they reached the top of the hill. Chad shifted down to a lower gear. They snaked down the road that suddenly narrowed. It was obviously less well traveled and led directly down to the river below. A few feet farther on, a neat three-foot piece of plywood had been nailed to a post anchored in the ground. Boldly painted on it were the words *Langdon Property, No Trespassing*. Chad took the fork to the left. The path was barely discernible in places, wide enough only for one vehicle. He pulled up by the side of the cabin.

Alyson jumped out quickly.

"I have some work to catch up on at the mine," Chad said, handing her the hamper Kate had packed. "How about I pick you up in a couple of hours? We'll both be hungry by then, anyway. And if I know anything about Kate, she's loaded you up with some wonderful food that would taste so much better with company present. I know a wonderful place for a picnic."

Before she had a chance to object, he continued on

blithely, "Fortunately for you, I happen to be free this evening too, so we can make an event of it. It would be a shame to spend your second night in the Land of the Midnight Sun alone."

Alyson hesitated, then nodded.

"Good. I'm glad that's settled. See you later." With a quick wave, he took off, leaving her in a cloud of dust as he spun the tires and set off the way they had come.

Alyson looked around her excitedly. As far as the eye could see, there was nothing but land undulating like some gigantic sea frozen in time. The tall, spindly spruce trees crowding each other in a frantic search for more space and sun had thinned out gradually on the drive there. The land now was a mass of dense, low-lying bush interspersed by patches of grass and clumps of brightly colored flowers. The delicate blue flowers Alyson recognized as forget-me-nots, but they didn't have the fragility she usually associated with them. Here they didn't grow singly, but clumped together, a huge bouquet. She bent down to finger the pale-green fronds of the plant at her feet. Sage. She had never seen the herb as it grew, but she knew the smell.

I must get a book on plants here, she determined. *I want to savor every part of this land.* "My land," she said aloud. "All of this property belongs to me."

She looked in the direction they had come. There was no sign of Chad or the camp. They were on the other side of the hill. Slowly she turned full circle until she had scanned the whole area. Not a living soul. Just one solitary cabin, the land, and the river. For a moment she felt a tightening in her stomach. She wished she had asked Chad to stay. The sense of being totally alone frightened her.

Stop being silly, she chided herself. *What on earth can happen to you in the space of two hours?* All the same, she knew she was glad Chad was coming back before too long. She turned to the cabin.

Her heart began thumping wildly, and a sudden panic spread over her. She had no key. No one had mentioned anything about a cabin to her. What would she do if the door was locked? And what on earth was she going to do for two hours if it was just an empty building?

Darn Chad Braeburn, she thought. *I'd never be in such a situation if it weren't for him. I'd have thought clearly, asked sensible questions, taken charge. Now I'm stuck here on my own, scared stiff because I don't know if this area is dangerous, probably locked out of my own darned place, and I'm dependent on him to come to my rescue.*

Hesitantly she walked up to the cabin and tried the door. The latch lifted easily. With a sigh of relief, she pulled the door open and walked in.

Chapter Four

"She really is attractive," Chad said aloud.

Once out of sight, he had pulled the truck to a stop immediately. After all, he really couldn't leave her in the middle of nowhere without being assured that she could, in fact, get inside the cabin. Now he regretted his rash behavior and wished he were standing beside her sharing in her obvious joy at arriving at the cabin.

He watched her reach down to caress the flowers that surrounded her. He felt a twinge in his chest when she suddenly started spinning around, arms outspread, like a dancing child. He had felt that same twinge several times during the past couple of days, and it had surprised him. It had been a long time.

Alyson was shouting something, and he strained to hear the words.

''My land . . . belongs to me,'' floated up to where he was standing.

The warmth he was feeling toward her was, in the next instant, shaded by a curtain of suspicion. *The land,* he thought. *Business. Money. Alyson has a way of making me forget about the real issue between us when I'm with her.*

He caught a last glimpse of her as she lifted the latch and stepped into the cabin.

He glanced once more through his rearview mirror as he drove slowly back along the narrow road. At the fork in the road he hesitated; then, instead of turning right to head back to the camp, he swung sharply to the left toward the river. There was a sheltered spot where he used to go to when he was a child visiting his father at the mine. It had been his secret retreat. He had gone there to gloat over some hard-won treasure from a classmate or to nurse his wounds when he needed space to work things out. It had been years since he had sat alone in that spot; today he felt the need to find someplace to sit and think.

The hideaway hadn't changed much. You could still settle yourself into the hollow mound of sand and watch the river placidly wend its relentless path along the base of the mountain. Above was the same clear-blue sky and, in the distance, the higher mountains, their tops capped with snow. *I wonder if some other miner's son has claimed this as his own,* he thought. He hoped he wasn't intruding.

Lying back against the soft, solid chair of sand, Chad set about the task of organizing his thoughts. Usually he went through this process as soon as he arrived at work each day, sitting down at his desk, pen in hand. For the first half hour no one was allowed to interrupt him. It was time he set aside for himself to list the tasks ahead of him for the day and sort them into an order of priority—must do today, would like to do today, can wait until tomorrow. His father had tried desperately to instill those work habits into him as a youngster, continually stressing the importance of determining what must be done and should be done and then doing it without regret and without hesitation.

Chad had thought the whole process absurd. He couldn't remember an exact point in time when he adopted his father's approach; it had sort of come along with the job. Now he was convinced of the efficiency of this course of action and constantly tried to persuade his foremen to take time off to organize before plunging ahead. Sometimes he felt he was beating his head against a brick wall, but he never gave up. He tackled problems in his social life in much the same way.

Without pen and paper handy, Chad found the points harder to pin down. Finding out about Alyson in order to get her to sell the land on behalf of her father was obviously a "must do." But the "would like to dos" kept sidetracking his ideas on just how he might accomplish his goal. He had enjoyed the ride in with her.

When Kate had called down at the café to find out if anyone would be willing to give Alyson a ride, he couldn't believe that fate had played so kindly into his hands. He suspected that Alyson would have given up the idea of getting out to Hunker's Creek that day if Kate hadn't come to her rescue. She certainly wouldn't have come down to the Eldorado and taken him up on his offer, he felt sure of that.

He grinned as he recalled the look of indignation on her face when he had arrived to pick her up at Cabin 3. At first he thought she would refuse to go; indecision had wavered on her face. Then good old Kate had come bustling in and turned the tables in his favor. He'd like to show Alyson more. Even though there had been a couple of tense situations, she'd been awed by the beauty of the land. He had watched her pale-green eyes positively light up with wonder as they eagerly devoured the scenery.

That eagerness warmed him. It felt good to share with someone who could appreciate the way she did. He sighed. Thirteen years ago he had first brought his bride to the Yukon. How he'd wanted her to be impressed by this land! What plans he had had for their future; for their children! But there had been no future, and there had been no children. The marriage lasted barely two years. At first Norah had tried, but in the end they both knew that she could never be happy here. The parting was bitter.

Chad met Norah at McGill University. She was in his first-year philosophy class. He noticed her immediately. Even on the first day, she had a group of friends around her. Her confident laugh could be heard above that of the others, and she talked and moved with a sureness that filled Chad with admiration.

When he arrived at McGill, he felt out of place and awkward. For the first time in his life he realized he had been born and raised in a small town. Even with the private schools he had been sent to, he had been limited to a compact, intimate circle of people. Now he stood on the outside, longing to become a part of sophisticated city life. Norah reveled in his naiveté. They went to nightclubs, the theater, exotic restaurants. And for three exciting, whirlwind years, they played the role of student by day and partygoer by night. They married in their final year, six months before graduation.

By the time university life was over, Chad had grown tired of the hustle and the bustle. He longed for the simpler life in his beloved Yukon. He remembered now how thrilled he'd been to be taking a wife back with him, how idyllic he had envisioned the family they'd planned together.

Each month he waited anxiously for the miracle to happen. When he'd suggested visiting a doctor, Norah had been angry. The day he found the birth control pills, he had to admit that something was going terribly wrong with their marriage. The row that followed became a pattern in their lives. Norah missed the city life. She cajoled, pleaded, schemed . . . anything to persuade Chad to move back to Montreal. In the end they both had to admit defeat. Chad had found his place, and he was unwilling to give it up, even to save his marriage.

After Norah left, Chad threw himself into his work to exorcise the guilt and the disappointment. Men who came from the cities to work for him found him a hard taskmaster. For the first six months they were on probation—"just to make sure this place is right for you and you're right for this place." It took almost five years for him to come to terms with the fact that his marriage hadn't worked and that neither he nor Norah was totally to blame. Norah had since remarried, and he was glad for her. He wished her well. He wondered now if she had any children.

Since that time Chad had been cautious. He knew most of the people in town and was able to mix readily with them. If he felt the need for company, he would go to the bar or pool hall, and then there were always the business trips. At the local dances and socials, people had grown accustomed to the fact that he came and left alone. Sometimes he was the butt of teasing remarks, but he found that he could divert their attention from himself easily enough with flippant retorts. Occasionally some well-intentioned souls would try to have a heart-to-heart. They were harder to brush off, for despite his irritation at their interference, he knew they meant kindly, and he didn't want to hurt their feelings. He remembered the time Kate had made him sit down at her kitchen table.

''What are you doing with your life, Chad Braeburn?'' she had demanded.

Before he'd had time to come out with some response, she had waved her hand at him to cut him short.

''Oh, don't come back at me with all your fancy talk. You don't fool me. I've known you since you were a baby in diapers. Your mother spent many hours in my kitchen, and if she were alive today, she'd sit you down and tell you what I'm going to tell you now. So don't you turn your charm on me and make my head spin with all your talk just so's you can get out of listening to the truth.''

Chad could see her now, viciously wiping at a coffee mug with her tea towel while staring at him with a fixed, determined expression on her face.

"Nobody's meant to go through this life alone. It ain't natural. Norah's gone, and nothing you can do is going to bring her back. She found herself what she wanted in life, so let it be. What's done is done. But that ain't no reason for you to hide away in that office of yours and work yourself to death. And don't tell me the mine can't run without you; your father built that mine from nothing and still had time to spend with a loving family. It's high time you took a good look at yourself, Chad Braeburn. If all you want out of life is money and power, then you ain't no Braeburn."

Chad shifted himself to a sitting position in the sand dune. Kate's words still echoed in his ears. Since that time, Kate had said nothing more about the subject. At first he had stayed away from her place, angry with her for saying to him so directly the words that he knew his mother would have said. Gradually he had resumed dropping in for an occasional coffee, but both kept the conversation on a general level.

Chad pursed his lips. "What the devil is coming over me?" he muttered. He stood up and kicked the sand at his feet. He looked at his watch. He would pick Alyson up in an hour. He wondered what she would be doing in the cabin. He grinned at the thought of her keeping an ear open for any sound of a grizzly. *She's probably scared stiff,* he thought. *A couple of hours on her own will be enough to make her glad to see me.* He was looking forward to the picnic. *We could take a detour on the way back,* he decided. *I could show her some abandoned prospectors' cabins from the days of the Gold Rush. Perhaps take a walk along the river.*

He could feel the excitement building in him at the thought of the two of them strolling along late at night with the sun still high in the sky. Perhaps tomorrow they could take his boat out on Alpine Lake and cook outside on an open fire. They could return to Dawson in time to get changed and go out for dinner at the Eldorado. The restaurant was one of the best in town, and they would be able to talk in comfort.

And just how am I going to fit in this business of selling the land? he mused. The thought brought him back to the problem at hand. Klondike Enterprises had expanded as far as was possible on the land his father had originally purchased. The precious metals in the ground were beginning to run low. Originally the government hadn't allowed land to the north of the property to be mined. When Harry Langdon had bought the land four years ago, it had been of little value to Chad, since laws regulated its usage. Now the law had changed, and Klondike Enterprises had purchased acres of land around the mine site. The only person who hadn't been willing to sell was Harry Langdon, and his property sat smack in the middle of the old mine site and the newly acquired land. Access there was impossible without trespassing on Langdon property.

Chad knew he was taking a bit of a gamble when he made the new purchase, but he hadn't anticipated someone refusing to sell the land if the price were high enough. For the last two years he had instructed his lawyers to make repeated offers to Harry Langdon, each one considerably higher than the last. Each time the lawyers had received a simple handwritten reply: *No, I am not interested in selling the land. Thank you. Harry Langdon.* The last offer had gone out over six months ago, but this time there hadn't been the usual response. In fact, there had been no response at all. Chad had interpreted that as a promising sign of consideration of the idea; he had certainly not expected a daughter of his to turn up as the negotiator.

Disconsolately, he bent down and picked up a smooth, flat pebble. He rubbed it contemplatively between his fingers, then crouched down and sent it skipping across the water. "Not bad," he said, as he counted the six splashes. It felt good to be outside with time to enjoy the open air. *It's about time I took a break,* he thought suddenly. *If Alyson is going to be here for three weeks, I could take time off and show her around. It'll give me a chance to find out what her plans are, so really I'd be working. At the same time, I can enjoy the pleasure of her company. After a week or so, I could explain the situation to her, and we could probably work out an acceptable arrangement. She could go back to San Francisco, and I could get working on future expansion in earnest.*

Oh, forget it! he thought. *Maybe I'll just enjoy her company for the next few weeks. I'll have a better chance of finding out what she's up to if I keep her in my sights.*

"You're breaking your own rules, Braeburn," Chad said aloud. "Don't mix business with pleasure—unless, of course, the lady is Alyson Langdon." A hint of a smile appeared on his lips as he turned toward his truck. He was suddenly looking forward to their picnic.

He'd have just enough time to go over to the mine and draw up instructions for paperwork in his absence before picking Alyson up at the promised time.

The local radio station was playing country-western music as he drove along. Normally he would have switched off the radio and put in a tape, but today the raucous, rollicking music appealed to him.

Alyson held her breath as she took her first step inside the cabin. Without warning, the strain of the past few months surfaced, and sobs overtook her.

"Oh, Dad," she murmured. "Dad. You're gone, and I don't understand. I'm so sorry."

Once again she longed to change the events of the past years. Disappointment at not even having made an attempt to understand her father washed over her. She remembered how bereft she'd felt the day he left the house so many years ago. It was the day after her thirteenth birthday. The words that he spoke that day were engraved in her mind forever. She could almost hear those words being spoken now.

"I'm sorry, Ally. I wish I could make you understand, but I know that you cannot." Her father had spoken the words with tenderness. "Just because I can't live here anymore doesn't mean that I'll stop being your father or that I'll ever stop loving you. I'm not leaving you, sweetheart, only the house. I pray you'll understand one day."

Oddly enough, deep down Alyson had understood why he was leaving. There had been bitterness in their house, albeit disguised, and the child had sensed it for years. Instinctively she had known that her father had no choice, but over the next few years, her mother had convinced her that she had been the one wronged. Her father's visits had become fewer and fewer—obviously the sullen teenager he visited didn't lend encouragement to more frequent visits.

Alyson escaped from her overbearing mother when she was nineteen, finally finding an apartment of her own. Working part-time, she had managed to put herself through college, ultimately landing her job at the nursing home. She had successfully dismissed thinking about her parents for several years as she went about establishing her career and a life of her own.

It was only after her mother's death three years ago that she thought seriously about her relationship—or nonexistent relationship—with her father. Perhaps it was because of her contact with her charges at the nursing home. So many lonely elderly people with no family who cared. Alyson had listened for years to the wonderful stories they told, and it brought to mind the wonderful stories her father had told her when she was a small girl. Stories of the Yukon. Stories always cut short when her mother entered the room. Alyson wondered why. What was his connection to the Yukon? Why was it a connection not shared by her mother?

Alyson had finally reached out to her father, and just when their relationship was blossoming, Harry Langdon had suddenly died. She hadn't even known he was ill. The thought of what could have been brought fresh tears to her eyes. Yes, she had deep regrets and couldn't change what had passed, but she now knew exactly why she had come here. Not because selling the property would have been too callous an act, but because she knew that it was here that the mystery of the past would be solved. Here, in the Yukon, in Harry Langdon's cabin.

The tears had a cleansing effect on her. She was suddenly filled with a sense of optimism. She rose determinedly and took in her surroundings. *I never dreamed of anything like this,* she thought. *It's just magnificent!* She didn't know where to begin; she merely stood anchored to the spot, drinking in the surroundings.

It was, in fact, a home—not the vacant, empty shell she imagined it would be when she first caught sight of it with Chad. It looked lived in. There were two huge windows running across the length of the large living-kitchen area. The view was spectacular. She imagined herself sitting on the deck that surrounded the entire cabin, taking in the scenery that she'd thought existed only in an artist's mind.

A shiny cookstove sat perched in the corner; pots and pans—they appeared to be hardly used—hung glistening in rows above it; logs were stacked in a neat pile beside it. An antique oak table with four press-back chairs took their place in front of one of the picture windows. Each chair had peach-colored woven seat covers that matched the deeper peach hues of the floral-print tablecloth. The cupboards were solid oak, obviously handcrafted—by her father? Grouped in front of the other window were two sofas and two comfortable armchairs, all in varying shades of peach and sea-green. Beneath all of this was a plush carpet, velvet green. The effect was stunning.

The cabin wasn't wired for electricity; coal-oil lamps stood on the end tables. Magazines were scattered on the round coffee table. She drew forward and picked one of them up. July, 1991. She felt butterflies in her stomach. So this is where her father had mysteriously disappeared last summer. He had merely told her he was planning a fishing trip up north. She assumed he was referring to Oregon. She smiled when she remembered how excited he'd been at what she thought then was an ordinary fishing trip.

So, beneath that fisherman demeanor was a man with a flair for interior design, Alyson thought.

The events of the years must have hurt him deeply. He obviously hadn't trusted her enough to share this part of his life with her. Would he eventually have? she wondered. Or did he feel that she would have mocked him, as her mother had throughout his life with them? She felt ashamed that she hadn't been stronger and wished that she had defended more valiantly this man, her father.

Alyson roused herself from her reverie and continued her appraisal of the contents of the cabin. A massive rolltop desk was positioned behind the grouping of sofas and chairs. It, too, was strategically placed so that one could take in the panoramic view through the windows. Antiques. She didn't know her father had a love of antiques. She resisted her urge to investigate the contents of the desk and, instead, continued to the back of the cabin, anxious to discover what the rest of the layout was like.

A large bedroom ran almost the length of the back of the cabin. A queen-size brass bed stood in the center of the room. Covering it was a quilt, similar in design to the one she had lain beneath at Kate's. She lovingly fingered the material.

Looking up, she found herself staring out yet another picture window, this one facing toward a dense thicket of jackpines set against a backdrop of snow-capped mountains. What a marvelous scene to wake up to! So different from the skyscrapers and smog she looked out on from her apartment in San Francisco. An oak dresser, night tables topped with coal-oil lamps, and a large wardrobe were the only other pieces of furniture in the room—all antiques. A braided area rug lay beneath the bed, lending further warmth to the pine floor and log walls. With a final glance she slowly moved out of the bedroom to the remaining room—hopefully, she thought, the bathroom.

It, too, was large; it, too, had a huge window overlooking the same scene as the one from the bedroom. "This is too good to be true!" she laughed.

There was a toilet, a vanity with sink, and, perched in front of the window, standing on brass claw feet, was the most fantastic-looking bathtub she had ever laid eyes on. Fluffy towels hung on the rack. This home was obviously ready for possession at a moment's notice. Suddenly she was struck by the thought that there might not be water. She tried one of the taps. Nothing. Perhaps there was some sort of a generator system. She vowed to ask Chad when he returned.

Good heavens! Chad! She looked quickly at her watch and couldn't believe that more than an hour had passed since she'd arrived at the cabin. And she hadn't really gone through any of her father's possessions, which would likely be in the desk and in various cupboards. She walked quickly to the front of the cabin and outside onto the deck. As her eyes swept over the valley below her, she made a resolution.

She raised her arms in abandon. *Yes, my father's! Mine! I'm staying here.* She was filled with excitement. *Why go back to Kate's when this is what I came for?* "Right, Dad?" she said mischievously. She whirled back into the cabin to take inventory of what she would need to bring back with her for her three-week stay.

Chad was taken off guard when he saw her appear suddenly on the deck. He could see her clearly from his vantage point. After rushing around the camp for the last half hour, all the while thinking of Alyson, he impulsively jumped into his truck to return to the cabin early. Once he got there, he felt foolish and decided to wait, out of view, at the same spot from which he had observed her earlier.

He was annoyed at himself for acting like some schoolboy with a crush. In an attempt to gain control of his emotions, he replayed the events of the past few days, concentrating on how they related to the business transaction he was trying to pull off. Try as he might, though, to analyze what had transpired between them, he kept falling off track. Instead, he could only focus on the warmth of her smile, the now familiar flashes of humor, the glimpses of sadness—all part of her charm. And once again here she was, dancing around like some schoolgirl, arms stretched toward the sky. Acting like a child, yet very obviously a woman.

He glanced for the hundredth time at his watch in an effort to calm the rush of emotion he was feeling.

It was precisely six o'clock when Chad knocked on the cabin door.

"Picnic time for teddy bears," he said, waltzing into the cabin without waiting for his knock to be answered.

Alyson jumped up from where she had been sitting and carefully folded the piece of paper she'd been reading. She blushed as his eyes met hers.

"Well, Mr. Braeburn, once again you seem to have taken me by surprise. You're probably itching to get your hands on this piece of paper to see what I've been reading this time," she chastised him haughtily.

"Really, Alyson, you do hold a grudge, don't you?" he said with a grin. "And it seems you've already forgotten our truce and have reverted to that horrible form of address. It's Chad, remember?"

"Even you, Chad, cannot ruin my mood. The past two hours have been wonderful. I've truly discovered the most marvelous place in all the world!" Her smile transformed her, and he was clearly puzzled.

"Come on," she continued. "It's enough for one day. Let's go to that wonderful spot you know and find out what goodies Kate packed. I'm starving."

She grabbed the picnic hamper and hurried him out of the cabin before he had a chance to take a good look around. In the fleeting glimpse he had of the inside of the cabin, he was struck by the number of books.

"Your father must be quite the reader," he commented, taking the hamper from her and steering her down the path toward the river. "I'd much rather walk, if you don't mind. It's not far from here."

"Dad used to read a lot to me when I was a small child. He had many books on the North even then. I bet I was the only kid in the ninth grade who didn't have to read *Call of the Wild* for an assignment." She laughed.

"I'll take you to Jack London's cabin tomorrow, if you like," Chad offered.

"Well, I was going to—"

"There'll be an actor there tomorrow reading excerpts from his novels and telling about his life. He's very good."

"But I thought I would get some things from town and—"

"He's really good. You might not get the chance again," Chad said persuasively.

Alyson hesitated.

"We could make a day of it," he continued, persistently pushing his advantage. "I thought you might like to go out on Alpine Lake and experience a cookout on the shore. And then there'd still be time to go out for dinner at a very nice restaurant in town," he finished in a hurry.

"You seem to have all this worked out."

"I'm sorry. I . . . er . . . I didn't handle that very gracefully. I've grown out of practice, obviously," he ended ruefully.

Alyson felt her heart lurch. "Well, one more day won't make much difference to my plans, I suppose." She could feel herself weakening. "I tell you what. If we get through the rest of today without any more confrontation, it's a deal.''

"Done," he said, grinning. "The path gets kind of tricky here. Give me your hand."

A moment later they were picking their way over masses of tree roots and loose rocks.

"This is obviously not one of the tourist spots." Alyson panted as they started to climb.

"Just up here," Chad said, a hint of amusement in his voice. "Come on, Cheechako, you can make it."

They stood at the top of the cliff overlooking the river below. Chad scanned the area, still keeping a firm hold of her hand.

"This should be good," he said, pointing to a grassed area ahead.

Alyson followed meekly behind. He didn't seem to notice she no longer needed his hand to guide her now that they were on solid ground. She could feel her heart beating wildly. His grip was strong and firm and re-assuring. She liked the feel of it.

"... and there's an old ghost town over there that still has a few prospectors' cabins remaining in quite good shape."

Alyson realized she hadn't been listening to Chad talking. With relief she silently thanked the gods he hadn't asked her a question.

His eyes laughed at her. He sat down on the ground and patted the space next to him.

"Let's eat, Alyson. I see a certain hunger in your eyes," he teased suggestively.

Chapter Five

"You watch out for Chad Braeburn, now," Kate said, clearing away the last of the breakfast dishes.

"Oh, Kate. You worry so. I'm quite capable of handling the Chad Braeburns of this world." Alyson tried to laugh lightly as she rose from the table.

"Yes, I think you are," Kate said, patting her arm. "That wasn't quite what I had in mind. It's Chad I worry about."

Alyson looked questioningly at her. Kate opened her mouth to say more, then resolutely closed it again.

"Never mind me, I'm just an old worrywart. You go and enjoy your day." The dishes rattled in the sink as Kate swished the water around viciously. "Will I be seeing you for supper?"

"Chad invited me to the Eldorado this evening. This morning we're going to listen to a reading at Jack

London's cabin; then we're going for a boat ride on Alpine Lake and to the restaurant in the evening.''

The noise of rattling dishes stopped suddenly. Kate turned to Alyson, then abruptly turned back to her task.

''Well, have a nice day now. I'll see what I can do about getting your supplies and such.''

Alyson could still hear the dishes rattling as she closed the door behind her and headed off for Cabin 3.

What a strange remark for Kate to make, she thought as she put the finishing touches to her hair. Laid out on the bed was her old faithful black dress. Thank goodness she had decided to bring along something ''just in case.'' The dress was simple but elegant. It had come to her rescue whenever she had wanted that something special. With her hair down loose and flowing and pearls at her throat and ears, the low-scooped dress never failed to produce a compliment. She was looking forward to today and wanted to impress Chad this evening. She had set the alarm so that she would have time to prepare her clothes in the morning. The alarm hadn't been necessary.

Even though it had been well past eleven o'clock when they had arrived back at Kate's last night, and midnight by the time Alyson had finally climbed into bed, she had lain awake, remembering the events of the day. Each time she closed her eyes, she saw the river, shimmering in the last rays of the sun, with Chad standing next to her. Occasionally he had taken her hand to guide her along the paths; occasionally his arm had rested lightly on her shoulder as he pointed to some distant sight. She could feel her body begin to tingle at the memory of it. One thing had been certain. Chad

Braeburn had proved to be an exciting man to be with. A man who had revealed so many sides to his character in so short a time.

Scenes from the picnic kept reentering her mind as she had lain tossing and turning, sleep eluding her.

Kate had packed a relative feast: chicken, potato salad, crisp vegetables, homemade buns, and an assortment of fruit. A bottle of Beaujolais complete with two crystal wine glasses had been her final touch. Alyson had been starving and devoured the food ravenously as Chad looked on appreciatively. After sipping a few glasses of wine, she didn't mind the teasing at which he was so expert.

"I pity the poor grizzly who attempts to take your food away, Alyson," he had mocked her gently. "Such a wonderful appetite for such a little thing! I suppose that was just hunger I saw in your eyes. Pity."

She had responded good-naturedly to his teasing. She was feeling a glow from the wine that was making her light-headed and reckless. "And just what makes you an expert on my appetite? Are all Yukon men such authorities on women, especially so soon after meeting them?" she had quipped.

"Not all, just some—me in particular," he had replied with feigned arrogance. "And only when confronted with a woman of such beauty." The dry humor didn't disguise the sincerity evident in his eyes. For a moment Alyson had wished that he would take her in his arms, but in the next instant she was shocked by her own thoughts. After all, she was virtually in the middle of nowhere with a stranger she had met less than twenty-four hours before. She would never have acted that way in San Francisco.

Alyson had managed to keep the conversation on a less personal level after that. The rest of the picnic had gone smoothly, both of them enjoying the scenery and the light banter. Chad seemed to have sensed that she was withdrawing from him on a personal level and adhered to her unspoken rules.

It was after eight by the time they had finished the picnic and explored the prospectors' cabins. Alyson reveled in the stories Chad told about the hardships the prospectors faced and was delighted that he appeared to enjoy sharing his knowledge with her. When they returned to the cabin, she had brought up the subject of water—or of what appeared to be lack of water—in the cabin.

"The cabin was obviously designed to have running water," she had commented casually as she gathered up her belongings. "I suppose Dad intended to have some sort of a system hooked up eventually."

Chad had explained that there was a generator system that would draw the water from the well and proceeded to give instructions on how to engage it. Alyson had listened with attentive innocence. She smiled as they left the cabin to set off on their trip back into town.

The scenery on the way back had been even more breathtaking than on the trip out. The midnight sun had cast a calm eeriness over the mountains and valleys. Alyson had drifted off to sleep, serene and exhausted, her head resting on Chad's shoulder. She roused herself from her deep sleep and forced herself to move away from the comforting nook when they arrived back at Kate's.

"Sweet dreams, Cheechako," Chad had whispered as they walked toward her cabin. He had brushed his lips against her forehead before turning to walk away.

At six o'clock Alyson switched off the alarm. She was eager and ready for the day to begin. She took a long, luxurious bath, savoring the memory of last night, eagerly anticipating the day ahead. Now she looked confidently in the mirror. She had plaited her long hair in a single braid that hung over her shoulder; in her jeans and sweatshirt she looked and felt like a young kid. The sweatshirt had teddy bears tumbling over each other in playful fashion. She doubted Chad would notice, but the selection had seemed appropriate. She chuckled to herself.

"Don't tell me," she called in response to the knock on the door. "Kate said somebody in Cabin 3 was looking for a ride."

"Not quite," a voice chuckled back. "Kate said a lovely lady in Cabin 3 was looking for a ride," Chad grinned, stepping inside. "And she was right. About the ride, I mean."

He ducked adroitly to avoid the well-aimed cushion Alyson threw at him.

They both laughed.

"So that's how you keep all your charges under control," he teased, grabbing her playfully around the waist. "I see I'm going to have to stay in shape with you around."

*   *   *

A number of tourists had already gathered at Jack London's cabin when Chad and Alyson arrived. Some stood around chatting idly as they waited for the performance to start; others had already settled on a piece of the lawn or were seated on one of the benches set out on the grass.

"This is drama Dawson style," Chad said.

They squeezed in next to an elderly couple on the benches. Alyson could feel the shape of Chad's leg next to her own. It seemed to her that all her nerve ends were exposed, putting out feelers to absorb more of his nearness. Suddenly everyone fell silent as a solitary figure emerged from the cabin. His voice thundered across the morning air as he began to recount his life as a hobo, a sailor, and a Klondike adventurer. Alyson pressed in against Chad as "Jack" began reading an excerpt from *The Call of the Wild*. His voice quavered with the passion and the fury of Buck's violent but memorable struggle to assert his right as leader of the dog team. Alyson gave an involuntary shudder.

"It's such a cruel book," she said later to Chad. "But there's something primitively noble about it that gives me goose bumps."

"I noticed," Chad said with a grin. "Maybe later this week we could take in a good old melodrama at the Palace Grand—just to show you the brighter, zanier side of Klondike life."

"When am I going to get my business done?" she wailed in mock despair.

"Well, not today, at least. Come on. We've got a whole lot of lake to see. I haven't taken my boat out

in years. Today I want to show her off like a boastful
schoolboy. I haven't had a chance to show off to anyone for ages, and I'm going to take full advantage of
this opportunity while I have it.''

He looks like a schoolboy, Alyson thought. Today
he had on jeans, a plaid shirt with sleeves rolled up to
the elbows, and a light-gray sweater thrown casually
over his shoulders. *Not half so intimidating as when I
first met him,* she admitted to herself.

''Here we are,'' Chad said. The lake glistened a
deep blue-green before them.

''There's no one else here,'' Alyson said in surprise.
''I've never been to a lake in my life where there
haven't been swarms of people on the shore and on
the water.''

Chad laughed. ''I forgot you're not used to this.
We're spoiled here. To us it's normal to be the only
ones on the lake. In fact, some people get downright
annoyed if someone else turns up to invade their pri-
vacy. If you consider that only 27,000 people live in
an area of 207,000 square miles, that averages out to
one person every eight square miles. We thrive on
space.''

Alyson watched as Chad expertly backed the boat
and trailer into the water.

''Don't lose the boat,'' he called, tossing a rope at
her. ''I'll be back in a minute.''

He drove off with the empty trailer behind, leaving
Alyson standing at the water's edge, with the boat
swaying gently back and forth in rhythm with the water.

She put her hand in the water as Chad came striding
over to where she stood.

"It's like ice!" she cried, feeling her hand tingle with the momentary contact.

"It takes less than five minutes in these waters for hypothermia to set in," Chad commented.

He took the rope from her hand and pulled the boat slightly up on shore. He had put on a pair of hip waders while he had been gone.

"I'm afraid we don't have docks here so that you can step elegantly afloat." He smiled, scooping Alyson into his arms.

She leaned against his broad chest, her heart pounding wildly as he carried her and lowered her gently into the boat. His eyes twinkled mischievously as he placed her in the seat. The water lapped around the top of his thighs as he guided the boat fully into the water. He scrambled on board.

"Hold on to your ponytail!" he yelled above the noise of the roaring motor.

Alyson felt the front of the boat lift in response to the open throttle. Behind them the water spewed a gigantic fan of spray as they sped down the length of the lake. The trees on the shoreline blurred, and she had to look past them to focus properly. She could feel the air racing past them. The rush of excitement made her feel light-headed; her skin prickled with the sensation. Chad stood at the steering wheel. The front of his shirt was flattened against his chest; the back billowed out behind, flapping with the speed. Gradually he slowed the boat down to a steady, quiet drone.

Alyson laughed. "Disneyland has nothing on this!" she cried breathlessly.

"It's exhilarating," he replied. "Everybody should

be allowed to go all out at times. To abandon oneself to the elements. To feel completely free. It does wonders for the ego.''

"Do you always live so dangerously?''

"Dangerously? Not at all. I know these waters. Look around you. What is so dangerous if you know and respect what's here? I think,'' he continued, resting his elbow on his knee and staring intently into her eyes, "you mean do I always live so passionately? Oh yes, I do if I can. If something is precious to me, it's worth any risk and any price.''

"Some*thing* or some*one*?'' Alyson heard the slight tremor in her voice. She kept her eyes fastened firmly on Chad's.

"Ah, you seek to probe the inner workings of my mind and soul. And then where would the mystery be?''

He settled himself into the chair beside her, then reached his arm across and gently trailed his fingers over her hair. Alyson felt the spreading warmth of the blush on her cheeks.

"Touché,'' she said lightly. "I see you're a master at sidestepping in our game of wit and repartee.''

"And you're better than I thought, Cheechako. Tell me where you learned your fancy steps.''

Alyson laughed. "Nowhere. I live a very sedate life. Most of the people I'm with all day find it hard to remember what day it is or what they said five minutes ago. There's little room for playing verbal acrobatics.''

"How can you enjoy working with people who are old and dying?''

"Sometimes it's sad,'' Alyson acknowledged softly.

Her voice grew husky, and she lowered her eyes. "Each time someone dies, the pain is still as strong. I still go home and mourn. You don't get used to death, no matter how often you see it.

"But there's so much I learn every day at the home. I love to listen to their stories—what life was like when they were young, what experiences they've had, how they've learned to survive. You know, most of them have such wonderful tales to tell and no one to listen to them. Their families often don't have time for them anymore, and I fill a void in their loneliness."

Gently Chad put his hand under Alyson's chin and tilted her head until her eyes met his. Then very slowly and tenderly he caressed her cheek. They fell silent for a while.

"I married thirteen years ago," he said, a note of sadness in his voice. "She was very precious to me. But not precious enough to risk anything or pay any price. She couldn't stay here, and I couldn't leave."

"Would anything make you leave here?"

"Nothing."

"And no one?"

"No one," Chad said steadily.

"And you never remarried?"

"I'm a hard man to satisfy, Alyson. I learned that about myself. I want it all. The land. The mine. Love and passion. A family. That's a pretty high order these days."

"The mine?"

For a moment he looked at her in confusion. He bit his lower lip.

"I'm a miner. I'll always be a miner," he said,

removing the hand that had been resting lightly on the back of Alyson's seat. "The mine has been my life. It means a lot to me, that's all."

He placed both hands back on the steering wheel. "But you're winning at our game. I want to learn more about you. What makes you tick, I wonder, Alyson Langdon?"

Without waiting for a reply, he slammed the throttle forward, and the bow of the boat lifted out of the water with the sudden burst of power.

"You mean you really didn't know there was a cabin on the land?" Chad frowned, reaching across the table to pour another glass of wine.

"Of course not. I said I didn't," Alyson replied, confusion evident in her voice. "Why would I lie? And why would you think I did?" she asked, clearly agitated.

"I didn't mean to imply that you had lied. I'm sorry, Alyson. It just seems odd to me that your father wouldn't have told you that there was a cabin on his property. Actually, more than a cabin, a house."

Alyson stifled her annoyance. The conversation was heading into a taboo area. She had merely commented that she, like the men and women who had come North in search of gold, didn't really know what she would find when she arrived at her destination. And that the cabin had been a pleasant surprise.

"No, Chad, I really didn't know," she said quietly yet firmly. "Now, I really am interested in hearing more about the Gold Rush. Tell me what happened when the stampeders reached Bennett Lake." She deftly diverted further discussion about the cabin. She didn't want to spoil the mood.

It was a few moments before Chad responded. His eyes searched hers for understanding. When none was evident, he leaned forward and rested his hand on hers as he continued the story.

Alyson tried to suppress the feelings racing throughout every nerve in her body and made a concerted effort to focus her attention on what he was saying. She had had to make that effort several times today and was finding it even harder now with his hand cupping hers.

She looked elegant in the black dress. This time her hair flowed loosely in soft waves that fell well past her shoulders. Her face was slightly tanned from being in the boat; the candlelight enhanced the glow of her green eyes. Several times she had stopped herself from staring at Chad throughout dinner. He looked even more handsome than before. His rugged features stood out sharply against the light beige shirt and tan sportscoat, his coal-black eyes sparkling devilishly in the flicker of the candlelight.

It had been an exhilarating twenty-four hours, beginning with the picnic yesterday. Such a mixture of activities—and emotions. The fact that she was physically attracted to him had been apparent to her from the moment she set eyes on him; what pleased her now was the fact that she truly liked and respected this man.

If only that unpleasant encounter on the plane hadn't taken place! she thought. And there, too, was the feeling that his questions about this business with her father were sometimes too pointed, too probing. For most of the day she had managed to suppress her gnawing doubts about his behavior and thoroughly enjoy his company.

"Alyson, *would* you?" She was jolted from her thoughts by Chad's pointed question.

"I'm sorry. Would I what, Chad?" She blushed, embarrassed at having been caught. Actually, she *had* been listening to what he was saying—at first. Then she'd started to focus on the way his features emphasized what he was saying, the way his mouth formed the words, the way his eyes displayed his emotions. She had been so busy paying attention to the physical him, she'd neglected to pay attention to the words.

"More wine. Would you like more wine?"

Her heart sank as she realized that he was aware of the effect he was having on her. His eyes positively sparkled with enjoyment. She made a quick effort to restore her dignity.

"No, thank you. Wine seems to have a dazzling effect on me. I think I've had enough." She smiled graciously.

"Well, I'm sorry to hear it's just the wine," he continued his gentle teasing. "I had hoped my presence would have dazzled you more than the wine." His disappointment was obviously put on, and she appreciated that, once again, he had used humor to release her from an otherwise embarrassing moment.

"Now, I've told you enough stories about the history of the Yukon," Chad breezed forward. "What about you, Alyson? Tell me more about your life in San Francisco."

Chad had found out very little about Alyson's per-

sonal life, even though they had spent the best part of
the last two days together. He had sensed several times
today that she had been on the verge of telling him
more about her reasons for coming to the Yukon, but,
for some reason, she always redirected the conversation
at the last moment. He couldn't press her for fear that
she would become even more suspicious of his behavior than she already appeared to be.

How did I ever allow myself to get involved in this
charade? It's just not my way of dealing with people,
Chad thought. He scorned others who toyed with emotions—others who didn't have the courage to deal with
a situation honestly. He had always made sure that all
his business transactions were above ground, all cards
laid on the table. It was a point of honor with him.
Now he was disgusted to find himself in the middle of
a relationship, one that had started out as purely business, clouded by deceit. How would he be able to
explain his conduct to her?

The day had gone so well. Chad had never dreamed
he could enjoy being with another person so much. He
was completely fascinated by Alyson's beauty and
charm—and adaptability. Last night he had been overcome with tenderness when she had leaned her head
on his shoulder and drifted off to sleep. She had looked
so vulnerable. When he'd stopped the truck at Kate's,
he had suppressed his urge to fold her in his arms and
cover her with kisses.

This morning she'd looked so fresh and alive. Anticipation shone from her green eyes. Her silky hair
was woven into an intricate braid that reached halfway
down her back.

This evening she presented a totally different image—all sophistication and glamour. Her auburn hair was unrestrained, a mass of soft waves resting seductively against the stark black of her cocktail dress. The contrast was stunning.

"I've worked at the nursing home for the past six years. At first I wasn't sure I had chosen the right career." Alyson stared pensively at the flicker of the candle as she spoke. "I couldn't seem to separate my job from my personal life in those first few weeks. Most of my charges appeared to be so lonely, so without hope. At least that's what I thought. I would leave work feeling helpless and full of pity for them. Until I finally realized that they weren't so desperate, really—they had created their own special family among the residents. They were actually less lonely than some of us who have family but make no attempt to see them—until it's too late."

Chad caught a glimpse of sadness in Alyson's eyes before she continued.

"I'm not sure when it happened, but those wonderful people made me a part of their family. They're all very special to me." Alyson smiled.

"Like your Grampa Hill who gives you very good advice about grizzly bears?" Chad interjected with a grin.

"Like Grampa Hill." Alyson grinned in return. She felt pleased that he had remembered their earlier conversation. "And old Mrs. Parsons," she added thoughtfully.

"And what advice did dear old Mrs. Parsons give you?" Chad replied, clearly enjoying listening to her.

"Just something about keeping my skin protected lest I get 'eaten alive by all them black flies and mosquitoes.'" Alyson stroked her skin dramatically as she replied, mimicking Mrs. Parson's tone. Chad laughed appreciatively as she added quietly, "Among other things."

"Oh? What 'other things'?" he challenged good-naturedly.

She raised her glass toward him and smoothly sidestepped the question. "Perhaps I will have another glass of wine."

"It's been a wonderful day for me, Alyson." Chad filled her glass, then reached across the table and took her hand once again in his. "There are lots of things I want to tell you about me, but I need time to think them out carefully before I say them."

Alyson held her breath.

"All I can say at the moment is that you're the most beautiful, exciting person I've known. Do you know how much willpower it has taken to stop myself from taking you in my arms and kissing you? When you fell asleep on my shoulder last night. In the boat today."

His eyes bore down into hers. The look was so intense, Alyson couldn't break the hypnotic power behind it.

"I don't know what to say, Chad. It's so fast. . . . You don't understand why I'm here. . . ." Her voice trailed off weakly. She stared helplessly at him.

"Spend the week with me, Alyson. Let's worry about business after that."

She could feel the increased pressure on her hand.

She willed herself to look away, and in that moment the spell was broken.

"What is it, Cheechako? Is business so important to you?"

She pulled her hand from his swiftly at the taunt in the voice.

"That's not fair, Chad," she said quaveringly. "Let's not spoil a lovely day, please."

She clasped her hands nervously in her lap. He leaned back in his chair and looked at her silently for a moment.

"Well, *is* business so important to you?"

"Yes, it is," she flashed back defiantly. "This particular business *is* important to me. . . . It's *very* important, if you must know. I didn't say I didn't want to be with you. I do. But I have to have time to think some things out. Tomorrow I'm going out to the cabin, and I'm going to stay there. If you want to come—"

"Stay there? You can't stay there by yourself," he cut in. "That's the most ridiculous thing I've heard you say. You're in the middle of nowhere there. You don't know the first thing about living here."

"Maybe I don't," she snapped. She could feel the blood rushing to her face and the tremor in her voice as her anger grew. "But I can make my own decisions, Chad!"

"Alyson, I'm sorry. Let's get out of here and talk things over. You're far too upset right now." He stood up and took the bill from the table. "I'll be back in a minute."

She watched as he headed off to pay the bill at the bar. *How dare he order me around?* she seethed. *He's the most patronizing, chauvinistic.* . . . Her mind grappled for adjectives to vent her anger. Tears of frustration gathered.

He will not see me break down and cry, she vowed. She got up hurriedly from the table.

When Chad returned, Alyson was nowhere in sight.

Chapter Six

Alyson put down the last of her father's diaries. She uncurled her legs from beneath her and got up from the sofa. Since last evening she had done nothing but read and reread the material she had found.

"What a mess we can make of our lives!" she said out loud. "Oh, Dad, why couldn't you say in person all the thoughts and dreams you wrote down on paper?"

She carefully placed the most recent diary she had been reading on top of the others and put them in the desk.

She had found the diaries in a box resting in the corner of the old wardrobe in the bedroom. She hadn't really been looking for anything in particular. She thought at first that they were books her father hadn't gotten around to putting on the bookshelves. But as she began to push them away, thinking that she would decide what to do with them later, she reached forward and picked one up. Her father's handwriting was on the cover—*July, 1991*. Last year.

She had stared at the writing, suddenly aware that what she was holding was her father's diary. She reached into the box again and drew out others at random—1983, 1987, 1988. At first she just sat on the floor, staring at the box in disbelief. *It will be here,* she had thought, *in these diaries.* Her father's life, contained in leather-bound books neatly piled in a box in a wardrobe two thousand miles from where she lived. In a part of Canada that she hardly knew existed until three months ago. She dragged the box into the kitchen and arranged the books on the table.

There were fifteen in all, the first one dated 1978, the year he left his wife and daughter. An hour passed before she found the courage to begin reading. Not that she didn't want to read them. She did. She just had to overcome the guilt she was feeling at the mere thought of it.

Dad would never have left them here if he didn't want me to read them, she told herself. *He knew he was dying and still left me this cabin with all his possessions in it,* she thought with more conviction.

Once she had made her decision, she sat down at the table and determinedly reached for the first diary.

Now, two days later, she'd finished. Now she understood her father's connection to the Yukon and why he couldn't banish it from his thoughts over the years. She stared once again at the faded photograph she held in her hands. A picture of a beautiful, dark-skinned woman—the woman her father had fallen in love with over thirty years ago.

It was six o'clock, and she'd promised Kate when she left with her supplies yesterday that she would be sure to eat lots and look after herself. She hadn't eaten since breakfast, and now that she had come to the end of her reading, she realized how hungry she was. For the first time today, too, she thought about Chad.

She couldn't remember distinctly what they had eaten at dinner at the Eldorado. Most of that evening was a blur. At first everything had gone so well. He had been witty and entertaining; they had held hands. Chad had told her how much he had wanted to kiss her.

"You're the most beautiful, exciting person I've known." The words had sent Alyson's head reeling. If they hadn't been in the restaurant, Alyson knew he would have taken her in his arms. She had seen the yearning in his eyes. She knew, too, that she was beginning to fall hopelessly in love with him, and there was nothing she had wanted more than to be held by this man.

The next minute Chad had started taunting her about business, pushing her to spend all her time with him . . . to forget the business she had to do.

"It's all me or nothing." That was the challenge he had thrown at her.

"But I have other responsibilities, Chad," she said now. "I can't put my father aside anymore."

If only I'd been able to tell you about Dad and why I'm here, she thought, *we could have found time for everything. But it wasn't the right time or the right place in the restaurant.*

Alyson set about cutting up salad greens to complement the cold chicken she planned to have for supper.

Her mind drifted back to the last scene in the Eldorado.

Why did he have to start being so dominating? Why did he think he had the right to oppose her coming out to her father's cabin, *her* cabin, if that's what she wanted to do? The anger she felt in the restaurant returned now.

"Of all the arrogant, chauvinistic. . . ." She stabbed at the tomato with the knife.

Suddenly she giggled as she thought of how furious he must have been when he returned to the table only to find her gone. She herself had been shocked by her behavior. After trudging the four blocks back to Kate's in high heels over the wooden sidewalks, down streets that were lit only by the rays of the midnight sun, her anger had cooled somewhat. Her attention had been directed more toward where she was placing her feet rather than toward the scene in the restaurant. She had half hoped he would come after her, but, knowing Chad, Alyson knew he wouldn't give in to her.

The next morning she had risen early and headed out to the cabin in the old truck Kate had managed to borrow for her. Alyson didn't want to chance running into Chad until she was on familiar territory—her territory. She couldn't deal with her feelings for Chad until she had dealt with the business of her father.

Chad had arrived at the cabin around noon, his features struggling to contain his anger and frustration.

"I told you it was foolish to ever think of staying here by yourself, Alyson," he seethed. "Stop acting like a spoiled brat. Abandoning me in a restaurant and trudging home by yourself is one thing. Now you've gone too far.'' His eyes bored through her as he stood in the doorway.

Alyson's eyes were glazed, almost devoid of emotion as she quietly, almost trancelike, responded to his words.

"Leave me alone, Chad. I want you to leave me alone for a while. Please go away.''

"Alyson, what is it?'' He stepped forward and tenderly placed his hands on her shoulders. "What's wrong, darling?'' he prodded softly. His hand cupped her chin as he raised her eyes to his, searching for understanding there. Alyson didn't hear his term of endearment. She wanted him gone.

"Chad, please. Just a couple of days. Please leave me alone.'' She leaned forward and rested her head on his shoulder, no longer able to meet his questioning stare. "Please, Chad.''

Chad overcame his desire to persuade her to confide in him. Instead, he held his body rigid, stroking her back in an effort to comfort her; then, for an instant, he brushed his lips against her ear and whispered, "Just for a couple of days. Then we'll talk, Alyson.''

With gentleness he pushed her away from him, turned, and strode out the door. It was the most difficult thing he had ever done, but he sensed that he wouldn't gain favor by forcing the issue. Alyson had a streak of stubbornness, he'd discovered, that he couldn't bully his way past. He'd found that out in the restaurant last night when she'd left him alone, looking like a fool.

Chad had been furious. He wasn't used to having

people walk out on him, especially women. His fury turned to concern when he realized that she was obviously going to walk back to Kate's. Dawson was safe enough, he supposed, but he still didn't want Alyson walking around by herself so late in the evening. He had followed her, keeping a discreet distance. At times he laughed at the picture she had made, dressed to the nines, trying to look perfectly normal striding down the boardwalk at eleven o'clock at night.

His laughter turned to annoyance when he realized he had to walk back to the Eldorado to retrieve his vehicle. She would have made it back just fine without his watching over her. That thought annoyed him. Alyson Langdon appeared not to need anybody. Chad admired her independence but felt a pang of regret at the realization that she could turn from him without so much as a backward glance.

When Chad arrived at Cabin 3 the next morning to smooth out the relationship, he had been shocked to find her already gone.

''She left bright and early this morning, Chad,'' Kate had informed him, peering at him steadily to gauge his reaction to the news. ''Figured you would have known that. Something amiss between the two of you?''

Chad drove faster than usual out to Hunker's Creek. He had been stung by Kate's flippant comment. He kept rehearsing the things he would say to Alyson when he saw her. This time he would . . . what? He floundered. As he approached the cabin door, he felt confident that he could take charge of the situation. He was so intent on saying his piece that when Alyson first opened the door, he didn't notice she was distraught. It was only after he made his rude comments that he noticed she'd been crying. Why she was crying wasn't evident.

Alyson had asked him to leave, and he knew that this time he had no choice. He had to leave her alone and would—until she decided to share with him the reason for her behavior.

Even though Alyson had requested a couple of days from Chad, she'd half expected him to turn up all day today. Now she tried to rehearse what she would say to him when he arrived.

"Please sit down, Chad. I have to explain why you made me so angry. My father died recently. . . ."

No, that was too stark.

"The last six months have been difficult for me. I'm trying so hard to come to terms with my father's death. I can't fall in love right now."

Nothing sounded right.

At seven o'clock there was still no sign of Chad. The first night Alyson had been too caught up in her reading to worry about being alone. Now that she had time to think about herself and the present, she was beginning to feel a little nervous. What if there really were bears around? Who would hear her if she cried out for help? She could drive back to Kate's in the truck her nephew had lent her for the week. But how would she get past the bear and into the truck, even if she had to?

Good heavens, Alyson Langdon. What on earth can harm you out here? she chided herself.

She ran the water in the bathtub. The bath had always

been her refuge. "When in doubt, have a bath—that's your motto," her mother used to complain.

She leaned her head against the back of the tub and stretched full length. The tub was so large, her toes barely touched the other end. She swished the suds of the bubble bath around, making a pathway with her hand to watch the bubbles flounder on their own before joining forces again. It was a childish game that had always fascinated her.

The rippling of the warm water against her skin gave her the sensation of gently drifting through space. She closed her eyes. She saw her father, young and carefree, as he was in the pictures with the young woman at his side. The two were obviously in love. He had his arm around her in a gesture that showed both tenderness and protection. She was looking up at him with adoration in her eyes.

The woman had no name. She was simply the "love" that her father had passed up in the name of sensibility. He had met her when he was twenty-two, a young man traveling in Alaska, taking odd jobs here and there, finally ending up in Dawson City, Yukon. He had fallen deeply in love with her the moment the two met. He hadn't asked her to marry him. The Yukon wasn't his home. His responsibilities lay with his family at home in San Francisco. It was expected of him that he would settle down and raise a family there with one of his own kind.

So he had thought to erase her memory and the passion he felt for her by returning home. He had married Alyson's mother shortly after and settled down where he belonged with a sensible woman.

But time hadn't erased the memory or the passion.

Even the arrival of my daughter Alyson could not fill the endless, aching need, he had written. *Knowledge came too late for me. I let my love go, thinking to find another as easily as the first. But some things are too precious and too rare to be offered twice. I did not look for my love. I did not know where to begin.*

"You shouldn't have given up, Dad." Alyson sighed.

The reference to the day he left Alyson and her mother had affected her deeply.

It is a selfish move to walk away from one's responsibilities. It is hard and shameful to admit that you've had enough. But leaving was the first honest act of my life. I wasn't the only one who didn't try hard enough. There was no one there to catch the tears I cried for us. In the end they became the tears I cried for myself.

Today I bought my land in the Yukon, the entry for March, 1987, started. *It is an unwise move. It lacks all sensibility. It is the best move I have ever made.*

Plans for building a retreat there were outlined in detail.

It will be the home I should have built for us. My love will never know of its existence, but it will be built for what should have been. It will be my salvation, for in the end I may finally find the courage to forgive myself for all I didn't do.

"You were too hard on yourself, Dad," Alyson said aloud.

She wondered if her father could see her now. She hoped so. The diaries had revealed a man of great sensitivity—a man she could now understand and accept with all his doubts and failings.

The image of the two lovers floated away. The figures blurred into one and gradually transformed into Chad's features.

"You are the most beautiful, exciting woman I've known."

Alyson saw Chad lean forward with the intensity of his emotion. His dark eyes softened with tenderness and longing.

Reluctantly she brought herself back to reality. Chad was obviously not going to come out today. Tomorrow she would go back into town and settle the business at the lawyers'. She would tell them of her father's death and her decision to keep the land and the cabin. It would be her haven to come to whenever she had the need to be alone.

She reflected on the letter her father had received from Dawson City. The money offered by Klondike Enterprises was mind-boggling; it would give her a kind of freedom she had never known or imagined before. But it would break the ties to her father's dreams—and now her link to Chad. She didn't know what the future had in store, but as long as she had a place in the Yukon, she had a link to two men who meant so much to her.

Once the legal aspect was settled, then she would find Chad. She couldn't talk about her father before; now she was ready. Her father had let his chance go by, but he had saved his daughter from making the same mistake.

"Well, Alyson," she said, wrapping the bath towel

around her and loosening the pins that held her hair up, "your father gave you more than most people are offered in a lifetime."

"Do you always talk to yourself?"

The voice startled her so much she had to stifle the scream that rose to her throat. She whirled around.

"Chad?"

"Were you expecting someone else?" came the reply through the bathroom door.

Almost sagging with relief, she steadied herself against the vanity.

"There was no reply when I knocked, so I just walked in," he continued. "Do you always take a bath with the front door unlocked?"

"I just forgot. I won't be a minute." Frantically she looked around her for something to wear. She hadn't brought fresh clothes in with her. She hadn't forgotten to lock the door, either. In the back of her mind she knew that she had left it open in case Chad arrived, then left without her knowledge. It was a silly, dangerous thing to do. She would have been horrified had any of her friends done such a thing in San Francisco.

"I locked the bathroom door," she said defensively. "I didn't think anyone would dream of coming out here."

Hurriedly she piled the clothes she'd worn that day into a heap and reached for the terry robe.

"Sorry," she said, emerging from the bathroom. "I was going to have an early night," she continued, in an attempt to explain her attire. "I'll just slip into some clean clothes."

"You look perfectly respectable to me." Chad eyed

her from the sofa. "I'd much prefer you don't go out of sight, if you don't mind. You have a strange habit of disappearing."

His face looked strained. *He looks as though he hasn't slept,* Alyson thought guiltily.

"Oh, Chad, I know I've behaved strangely. There *is* an explanation, really."

"I'd love to hear it," he replied tensely. "In fact, I refuse to leave here until I do. I tell you how I feel about you. I pour out my feelings and pretty well make a fool of myself, and you tell me that business is more important than spending this week with me and that I have no right to be concerned about your being out here alone. I think it's time we both laid our cards on the table."

"Chad, that's exactly how I feel," she said excitedly, wrapping the bottom of her robe around her legs as she sat on the armchair opposite. She looked at him in thankful relief that he had come. She could see that he was serious; his eyes weren't twinkling, nor was there the yearning she had seen before.

In its place was a kind of sadness and a look of defeat.

Chapter Seven

Alyson finished her story.

She told Chad of her father's death, her inheritance, her desire to understand the hold this land had on the man she had loved so much but known so little. She told him of the diaries and her father's love for a woman that he, in the foolishness of youth, had lightly cast aside.

"Listen, Chad!" she cried, running to the desk and returning with a diary dated 1975. She seated herself beside him and impatiently flicked the pages until she found the entry she was seeking.

" 'Knowledge came too late for me. I let my love go, thinking to find another as easily as the first. But some things are too precious and too rare to be offered twice.' " There was a catch in her voice as she read. The words blurred on the page.

98

"And this, 'Even the arrival of my daughter Alyson could not fill the endless, aching need.'" She looked at Chad, her face animated, her eyes shining with love.

"I think," he said, taking her hand in his, "that I would have liked your father. It takes a man of great passion and courage to write with such intensity."

Alyson looked at him with gratitude.

Tentatively, he stroked her hair. The relief that had flooded through him when he realized why she had come to the Yukon sapped him of strength for the moment. A wild happiness coursed through his blood and set his heart pounding.

"So that's why you came here? Why you didn't sell the land right away?" Chad held her hand more tightly in his own.

"I didn't know why exactly. I couldn't put it into words. I just felt it was the right thing to do." She turned to him in excitement. "And it *was* the right thing to do. When I read all the things my father had to say, I felt he was talking to me, telling me to follow my feelings.

"If I'd sold the land, I would never have known about the cabin. I might never have understood my father. I'd never have met you. I'll never sell this land now, Chad. Never. It means too much to me. I'm a part of all of this, just as my father was."

The look in her eyes was unmistakable. They shone with relief and pride and a burning desire to share with Chad all the love and emotion she had so carefully controlled before.

"Alyson—" he began. But he couldn't go on. She had laid her cards on the table—just as he had said she should. But he couldn't find the words to explain his own actions.

What do I do now? he thought. There was no mistaking the fervor in Alyson. Her whole being was filled with emotion. He could see it; he could feel it.

It's not fair, the voice in his head persisted. *But she's not after money—it can all be sorted out.* The thoughts danced wildly in his head.

"Alyson—" he began again. But he couldn't bring himself to talk of land and business. He brought her hand to his lips. "Cheechako. My darling Cheechako," he murmured. Tenderly he placed his arm around her and drew her to him.

Alyson closed her eyes and abandoned herself to the warmth of his embrace. For the first time since her father's death, she felt whole.

The few hours' sleep served Chad well; he felt as alive and fresh as the early-morning air. Nothing could dampen the strong sense of optimism that today was going to be the most important day of his life. Somehow he'd be able to explain himself. Somehow. . . .

Noiselessly he lifted the latch to the cabin door and peered inside. There was no response to his gentle call.

"Darn that woman and her open doors!" He shook his head in resignation and grinned.

Alyson didn't waken when he called her name again, nor did she stir when he stood beside her bed. Chad looked at the hair spread out like a halo on the pillow. He reached instinctively to touch it, then slowly drew back.

He stood there for a moment longer, looking down

at her as she slept. He bent down to kiss her, then stopped himself and walked resolutely away. At the door he hesitated; then, without making a sound, he opened the latch and let himself out.

Chad walked toward his truck, changed his mind, and put the keys back into his pocket. *A walk will do me good*, he thought. *And at least Alyson will know I'm somewhere around if she wakes up and sees the truck.* He set off at a brisk pace toward the river.

The turn of events last night had thrown him completely off balance. The last thing he had expected to hear was that Harry Langdon was dead and that Alyson had come not as a business negotiator but as a loving, caring daughter. The incredible outpouring of emotion had left him at a loss for words.

I should have stopped it, he told himself. *Why didn't I tell her I was the one who wanted to buy her father's land?*

Chad knew the answer even before he finished the question.

Because, Chad Braeburn, he admitted, *you want her. You wanted Alyson the moment you set eyes on her. Last night she trusted you, and you couldn't risk losing that trust.* He kicked the dirt at his feet.

"I'll never sell the land, Chad, never!" Alyson's words floated back to him. He saw the image of her face so full of intensity and emotion.

He stopped dead in his tracks. He felt the same surge of wild exhilaration that he had felt when she'd said those words. Whatever else those words implied for his business, they were an assurance to him that she loved this land—could be a part of it. Could be a part of his life!

His mind seemed to explode with the possibilities that screamed at him. They could live in town, and he'd build her another cabin—move this one if she insisted. The mine could expand. There would be children, someone for him to pass on the legacy.

I've done it! he thought in jubilation. *I've got it all— the land, the mine, love and passion, a family. I never thought it possible, but I've got it!*

He ran back to the cabin, his heart pounding.

"Marry me!" he yelled, running and shouting at the same time. "Marry me!"

The door of the cabin burst open.

"Marry me," he panted, leaning against the door frame to catch his breath. "Will you please marry me, Alyson-beautiful-Cheechako Langdon?"

The coffeepot Alyson was holding tipped downward as she stared in astonishment at the figure before her.

Chad moved quickly to her side, took the pot from her hand, and set it firmly on the stove. "Marry me," he repeated, grasping her by the shoulders.

"I . . . I was just, just going to make some breakfast," she stumbled.

He put his hand under her chin and turned her face to his. He held her there, gazing unwaveringly into her eyes.

"Say you'll marry me," he pleaded softly. "Come live with me. Here in the Yukon. As my wife. Please."

"Oh, Chad." The look of adoration in her eyes was all the answer he needed. "What about breakfast?"

She mumbled faintly as he picked her up in his arms and twirled her around the room.

"Breakfast! I can think of nothing I want more than breakfast with you," he laughed as he finally set her down. He did not relinquish his hold on her, nor she on him.

"I fell in love with you the moment I saw you," Alyson said shyly. "But I couldn't believe it—that something so wonderful would happen to me."

"You're the most wonderful thing that has ever happened to me," Chad told her. "Remember on the boat when I told you I never remarried because I was a hard man to please? I meant that. But I promise you, my love, you will never regret marrying me. I'll build for you the house of your dreams. Your father would approve of that, I'm sure."

Alyson's eyes shone.

"And we'll have children. Lots of children. You do want children, don't you?" he asked, a sudden look of anxiety crossing his face.

"Oh, Chad," Alyson laughed, "of course I want children! But you're getting carried away. All I want for a time is to have you all to myself. You look so serious."

"But this *is* serious. We have to sit down and discuss our plans—make arrangements for our wedding, plan for your future, settle business at the lawyers'. . . ."

"Chad Braeburn, you're impossible!" she said in mock reproach.

"But I have to discuss business with you, Alyson. We have to settle our business before we. . . ."

The rest of his words trailed away as Alyson firmly pulled him toward her and stilled his mouth with kisses.

"One week. That's what you said," she whispered between kisses. " 'Spend this week with me.' That was your offer. And I accept your offer. This will be the most selfish, glorious week of my life. So, no business talk. Promise me you won't talk of anything but love for this one week."

Chad groaned.

"Promise, Chad."

"I promise," he said.

Alyson didn't see the fleeting look of worry cross his face.

"Where did you learn to cook so well?" Alyson asked as she watched Chad slice bread and toss the salad while two steaks sizzled in the pan. He uncorked a bottle of wine and poured each of them a glass.

"I've been on my own a long time. Besides, even workaholics like me need to have a hobby of some kind to unwind. Cooking kills two birds with one stone—I enjoy doing it, and I get to eat."

He raised his glass in salute.

"Here's to us and the wonderful relationship ahead," he said, clinking his glass against Alyson's.

She sipped her wine contemplatively. "What kind of nursing opportunities are there here?"

"Nursing? Well, none, really. There's no hospital here. People go to Whitehorse for that kind of service. There's a public-health nurse." He looked at her intently. "But I don't think she'd be overkeen on the idea of giving her job up for you, if that's what you had in mind.''

''I was just wondering,'' Alyson murmured.

The meal wasn't elaborate, but it was delicious. They chatted generally about food as they ate: their likes and dislikes, their specialties and their disasters.

Suddenly Chad set his fork down on the plate. ''I know we said we wouldn't talk business,'' he began seriously, wiping his mouth with his napkin and taking a gulp of wine, ''but we should discuss money matters. Unless you want to work, there would never be any need for you to do so. Ever. I have a lot of money, Alyson. I—''

''But I want to work, Chad. For a while, anyway. Besides, I'm not marrying you for money. I have far greater ulterior motives.''

He laughed. ''You never cease to amaze me, Cheechako. And I thought you the creature of innocence, while underneath that mantle of shyness lies a brazen creature, throwing herself at the first eligible male to come along.''

''You are *not* the first eligible male to come along,'' she responded indignantly. ''I've had my share of opportunities. It's just that I'd never found the right man in the right place before.''

Chad twisted the stem of his wineglass in his fingers. ''This is the right place for you, Alyson, isn't it? You're sure of that, aren't you?''

''Of course I'm sure, Chad. I told you I'd never sell this land, and I meant it.''

He set the wineglass back on the table. ''But that was before we talked of marriage.'' He looked at her in concern. "We could buy land in town, build a house there. Any design you choose."

"What's the matter, Chad?" Alyson laughed at him. "Whenever we mention my father's property—*my* property," she corrected herself, "you get all flustered. That's the second time today you've brought up business, and you promised one week of selfish indulgence."

Chad said nothing.

"There are three more days to go," she continued, coming to where he sat and placing her arms around his neck, "and I refuse to spend any more time on discussions of money and land. Besides," she teased, "I can always think about land when I'm tired of thinking about you."

She laughed gaily at her own remark, gave him a quick peck on the nose, then busied herself clearing the table.

"I'll race you to the river," she cried. "Last one there does the dishes."

She was already out of the door and well on her way before Chad had a chance to stop her.

Chapter Eight

The embers burst into brilliance as Chad added another log to the bonfire. Alyson was mesmerized by the dancing flames.

I feel as if I've been plucked from chaos, she thought, *and transported into a dreamworld full of beauty and happiness. There's no other place in the world I'd rather be, no other person in the world I'd rather be with.* Her eyes filled with tears as she thought of her good fortune.

"Your romantic trysts never cease to amaze me, Chad!" Alyson smiled up at him from the blanket she sat curled upon. "An evening picnic, complete with wine, in front of a roaring fire. I love it, darling."

Chad's look was full of tenderness at her childlike appreciation for the simpler things in life—the things that were also special to him. She stretched her arms toward him, beckoning him to come closer. He sat beside her and snuggled her against him.

"I've been thinking more about Dad today, Chad. About the hopelessness that must have tormented him all those years. I've seen patients at the nursing home who have resigned themselves to a life of hopelessness—accepting their lot in life, living in their self-made prison, nothing to dream for or hope for. I don't think there's anything that frightens me more than hopelessness. I'm sorry that Dad let his happiness pass him by, but I'm happy and proud that he finally grasped hold of a new dream that eased some of his sad memories, something that restored purpose to his life—this land."

"Your father was happy these past few years," Chad replied soothingly. "Proof lies in his diaries."

"All my years with you will be happy," she said with a catch in her voice. "There will be no regrets, ever."

"Would you really miss working terribly if there's no job for you here?" he asked. He stretched himself out full length beside her on the blanket and thoughtfully twisted strands of her auburn hair in his hand.

She turned toward him, her face close to his. "Yes, Chad, I think I would. Times have changed so much. There are still some girls who grow up with the notion of marrying someone who will take care of them financially so that they can stay home and raise children and be a dutiful and obedient wife. But I've never thought of myself that way." She reached over and kissed him lightly on the nose. "I'm too independent.

I like to come home at the end of the day feeling I've accomplished something.''

"And housewives and mothers who stay home don't?''

"Some do,'' she admitted. "From the little you've told me about your family, your mother probably really enjoyed doing what she was doing. And that's wonderful. I'm just not sure it would be enough challenge for me.'' She looked at him anxiously. "You don't like the idea of my working, do you?''

"It takes time to change old habits,'' he said, grinning and putting his arm around her possessively. He thought of Norah and how threatened he had felt when she kept looking for a job. And in the end he had still lost her. He didn't want to make the same mistake twice.

"What if you could find a job in the mine?''

"What kind of job?''

"I don't know. Something in the office at first to learn about the mine's operations. Once you got familiar with the company as a whole, perhaps you could take courses in business management and eventually move into a management position.''

"Are there any women in management there?''

"Well, no,'' he admitted sheepishly, and, when she pulled a disapproving face, added, "Perhaps it's time for Klondike Enterprises to take a new approach.''

She raised her eyebrows.

"Not that we've turned women down,'' he said defensively. "We haven't exactly had a horde of them knocking at our door.''

"That might be a challenge. I can type, I'm well

organized, and I enjoy working with people." She turned excitedly to him. "I can't believe it. One week ago I was thinking my life was all sort of set—living in San Francisco, working at the home, eventually meeting someone to share life with. And now look at me. I'm making plans to live in a different country, I'm contemplating a career change, and I know the very person I want all to myself for the rest of my life."

She leaned her head in the crook of Chad's shoulder. Being close to him like this, she felt as though nothing could spoil their future together.

"Are you sure, Alyson, really, really sure about all this?"

He looked at her intently. A fleeting look of worry creased his brow. She had noticed that same look a number of times lately. But it lasted only for a moment. Whenever he turned to look at her, the familiar lopsided grin emerged.

"Yes," she said gravely. "I'm really, really sure."

They kissed tenderly.

Each morning for the past week Chad had arrived at the cabin to take Alyson on a different adventure. They had gone fishing in the clear, cold waters of a northern lake, surrounded only by spruce trees and mountains. She had tried not to squirm as he expertly took the fish off the hook and stopped its thrashing around in the bottom of the boat with one quick blow. They had baked it on an open fire on the shore of the lake, sharing the sense of timelessness.

They had walked through brush where cranberries and blueberries would soon be in abundance, along the water's edge, watching the sun rise and set within the same hour, and to the top of a mountain where the land below stretched in endless beauty.

Top of the World. It was an apt name for a highway that offered a panoramic view of the earth as far as the eye could see. The two of them had stood hand in hand, gazing in awe at the mass of land spread before them, land that no man had ever set foot on, offset by mountains that had no names and rivers that wound their icy way from the glaciers that fed them to the wilderness below.

They had reveled in each other's company, learning about each other. The week had been exciting and intense.

Alyson drifted off to sleep, future plans fluttering through her mind. Perhaps they would even decide to live in the cabin. Maybe they could expand it—for their children.

Chad could tell by Alyson's breathing that she had fallen asleep. *It's no wonder she's exhausted,* he thought. *For the past week she's been racing around like a child on Christmas morning—bubbling with excitement, wanting to experience everything.*

Many times during the past week Chad had tried to bring up the subject of the land; every time Alyson had thwarted him. He was thankful now that she had. The bare truth would have exposed him as being calculating and somewhat ruthless. And, for sure, untrusting. He had cast Alyson as villain, and no matter how he would have tried to explain, nothing would have softened that accusation.

But last night Chad's plan had suddenly appeared

before him. It filled him with a sense of excitement and hope. Yes, he would tell Alyson the truth—he had to. He couldn't risk losing her because of deceit. The challenge now was to tell her the truth and to convince her that it was only love that had prevented him from laying his cards on the table sooner.

Mentally he rehearsed his plan. First, go to the lawyers and withdraw the offer to purchase the Langdon property. Instead, have his lawyers sign over to Alyson ownership of the property to the north. This would be Chad's wedding present to Alyson.

Next, make her a full partner of Klondike Enterprises. He knew that it was important for her to work. Besides, he had learned from his mistakes with Norah and was determined not to repeat them. It would be unfair to expect Alyson to sit at home—she'd made it clear that her career was important to her. He hoped that she would look favorably upon starting a new career—mining magnate. He smiled to himself as he pictured her in her new role. She could focus her efforts on developing the new branch of the mining operation on the property to the north. He would help her to learn. They could do it together.

Alyson, the land, children—all he wanted in life. Tomorrow night he would take her to the Eldorado to celebrate. Everything would be in place by then.

Chad felt Alyson stir. "Wake up, teddy bear. Time to go home," he whispered.

The next morning Chad awoke early. He was excited to set his plans in action and had much to do before he could effect them.

After breakfast with Alyson, he broached the subject of business. They had had their week; he could not put off the question of the mine any longer.

"I have to go to the mine to take care of business today. You *do* remember business, don't you? After all, I am a working man," he teased. "But tonight will be our special night together, Alyson. Candlelight dinner at the Eldorado. This time, my fleeing princess, I trust the ending will be quite different."

She burst out laughing. "Rest assured, dear Chad, I will never take flight again—unless, of course, you press me too far." The seriousness she attempted to convey in her voice was betrayed by the mirth in her eyes.

"Seven o'clock," he murmured. "I'll be here by seven o'clock."

He brushed his lips quickly over her forehead. He couldn't risk kissing her fully—he knew he would stay if he did. Today was too important. He couldn't allow love to impede the business he must see to. But tonight—that would be a different story. He would be able to tell her the truth at last.

Smiling in anticipation of what would be, he strode from the room, his mind already beginning to cloud with the business at hand.

Alyson watched him as he walked with purpose away from her. A smile still lingered on her lips. She stretched, catlike, contentment oozing from her body.

"You'd better be careful, Alyson Langdon," she said with a chuckle. "Pretty soon you'll start purring like a cat."

* * *

A germ of an idea had been taking shape in Chad's mind over the last few days. He grinned to himself now as he drove to his office. It was another warm, sunny day, and the breeze through the open window felt fresh and invigorating. He himself felt young and alive. The excitement of sharing with Alyson the pleasures he so much enjoyed had had a rejuvenating effect on him. All he needed now was to sit down and work out the details of his plan.

Last week he had promised Alyson one week of selfish indulgence with no business talk. But the week was over, and much as he had enjoyed every minute, he was relieved that the time had come for him to tell Alyson of his work at the mine and his plans for the future.

The idea had come to him as he lay with Alyson in his arms on the open shore. Each day the two of them had seemed to grow closer together. No matter what they did, there was a magic to it. The feelings that he'd had for Norah paled in comparison to the love he felt for Alyson. But the fear of losing her harped at the back of his mind like an irritating insect that refused to go away.

Dear God, don't let me botch this up, he had pleaded silently.

Thinking about the mine as Alyson lay in his arms, he realized that she could work beside him as his partner. She had a sharp mind. He had seen that as she talked about her nursing career; she would be excellent with people. But she needed her own space; a token position would be an insult to her and create havoc with his workers. The solution he proposed was simple.

If he were to sign the land to the north over to her, she would own almost half of the land Klondike Enterprises had acquired. The mine could expand through Harry Langdon's property and beyond.

It might be a little tricky convincing her to move the cabin, he mused, *but surely she will see this as a wonderful opportunity for both of us. If I give her the land to the north, she'll know that I'm not marrying her for the land. Heavens, that piece of property is worth ten times her father's!*

Seated at his office desk, he reached for a piece of paper and rapidly wrote down all the points he wished his lawyers to include in the agreement. Tonight he would give Alyson the papers, all legally signed and documented. Satisfied with the details, he resolutely picked up the phone.

Sally answered on the second ring.

"Hello, Sally. Chad Braeburn here. . . . Fine, thank you. . . . Put me through to Jim, will you?"

"Certainly, Mr. Braeburn. One moment, please."

Two minutes later Chad leaned back smugly in his chair. He enjoyed a little intrigue, and he chuckled to himself as he imagined Jim puzzling over his intentions. He hadn't told him of his plan; he had merely asked how long it would take for a contract to be typed up, ready for signature.

"I'll have everything worded exactly as I want it," Chad had told him. "I just want your promise that if I drop it off by four o'clock today, it will be ready for me to pick up by five."

That would give him just enough time to pick up Alyson.

Chad could just envisage the scene tonight. Alyson would probably wear the black dress she had worn before—she could hardly have packed a whole wardrobe of special-occasion wear for a vacation in the North—her hair would fall in long, silky waves over her shoulders. She would look tantalizingly sophisticated and alluring. He could see her emerald eyes sparkling with laughter, enthusiasm—and the wine.

At the opportune time he would hand the papers over to her. She would stare in disbelief at the fortune she was holding in her hands. Then she would look at him in gratitude, her eyes speaking acknowledgment of the enormity of his love for her. He would hold her hand and carefully explain why he hadn't told her at the beginning that he was the owner of Klondike Enterprises. She would understand. There would be no more hiding of the truth from each other ever again. They would be ready to start their life together.

Looking at his watch, Chad calculated he had a couple of hours to check on affairs at the mine. He wanted to make sure the week had gone smoothly. If he left the mine at two, he could get to town by four. While Jim and Sally prepared the legal papers for him, he would have enough time to select a present for Alyson.

He had no hesitation about what he would buy. He grinned as he remembered sneaking up behind Alyson as she stared intently at the gold nuggets on display in the jeweler's window. How easily she had blushed, and how drawn he had been to her even then! A gold-nugget necklace and earrings would say everything.

Reluctantly he put thoughts of Alyson out of his

mind and concentrated on the work piled up on his desk in front of him.

"It'll all work out," he told himself.

This time there was real confidence in his voice.

Alyson hummed happily as she straightened the cushions on the sofa and set about rearranging the photographs and ornaments her father had scattered about the room. She picked up the photograph of her father and his unnamed lover and propped it beside a framed picture of herself.

"You'll always remind me that nothing is more important than love," she said to the two of them. "I'll never make the mistake you made, Dad."

It occurred to her how coincidental it was that she and her father had both found love in the Yukon. Both in a way had been faced with the same kind of choice. Her father hadn't been able to surrender to the instinctive power of love; reason had triumphed over passion. She had deliberately ignored the nagging voice of reason that kept telling her it was all too fast, too impetuous.

Too darned spooky, she thought. *Sometimes I wonder if I'm really me or if this is all some reenactment of a scene that I'm playing out for the ghosts of yesterday.*

Even now as she thought of Chad, she could barely restrain her excitement. *No matter where we had met,* she convinced herself, *I would have had the same reaction.* That first touch on the shoulder on the plane had electrified her. He had unnerved her and provoked her anger at the slightest instance, she understood now, because she felt swept along by emotion that was out of control. All the same, she knew deep down that her father's love affair and the cabin built as a tribute to love also added to the romance and the excitement.

"I know I want to marry Chad," she said to the photograph. "But I just need a little time to myself this week—to separate Chad and Alyson Langdon from her father and his lover."

Thank goodness Chad had no other influences working on him. He had nothing playing a powerful role in his life that would make him fall hopelessly in love with a complete stranger. No yearning to fulfill a father's dream. No romantic, sentimental messages weaving a charm around him. Nothing other than Alyson Langdon, pure and simple.

She was looking forward to dinner tonight. She would enjoy being seen in public with Chad—without any dramatic endings this time. She was also looking forward to seeing Kate. They could go there after dinner and tell her their big news.

"Kate. Oh, my goodness!" Alyson suddenly remembered the truck she had borrowed from Kate's nephew.

She had promised to return it by the end of the week. Frantically she ran through the last few days in her mind. How many days had she had the truck? The time spent with Chad had been one long, glorious span of time that didn't readily translate into days of the week. Carefully she backtracked over the events that had happened since she had come to the cabin, and then with a sigh of relief realized she had one day left.

Whew! she thought. *I've got to get things back in*

perspective. I can't put everything off and let time fly by like this. There are so many things to arrange now— my resignation, arrangements for the apartment in San Francisco, straightening things out with the lawyers here. After all, that's why I came, and it's not fair to keep Klondike Enterprises wondering about their offer to purchase the land.

She checked the time. It was quite early, barely eleven o'clock. She could go into town and settle the matter with the lawyers once and for all. That would free her from worrying—or forgetting—about them the rest of the time. It would also give her a chance to drop in on Kate, pick up her black dress for the evening, and check about the truck. If Kate needed it by tomorrow, she and Chad could take two trucks back into town on the way to dinner and simply drop the nephew's off later that evening. If she was willing to lend it for a longer period, that would give Alyson the chance to travel around a little on her own while Chad was at work next week.

And I have to emerge from this cocoon for a while. Otherwise I'll have nothing respectable to tell old Grampa Hill and Mrs. Parsons. She smiled to herself as memories of their time together floated before her. *Hardly what they'd expect of me,* she thought, grinning impishly.

The drive into town was glorious. Early morning seemed to be the time for wildlife to make their debut. Two moose, a black bear, coyotes, porcupines, rabbits, and more rabbits watched her pass with little concern. Streetlights, street signs, cars, and more cars were the only things to intrude on her thoughts when driving along San Francisco's streets.

Alyson remembered how intimidated she had felt when she first arrived in the Yukon—actually, from the time she left Vancouver. She was amazed that it was such a short time ago that she felt like such an outsider. Now she would be a part of this land and of its people.

"The farness that fills you with wonder; the stillness that fills you with peace," she recited Robert Service aloud. *Yes,* she thought. *He captured the essence of this land in those few words. I feel at peace.* She vowed to read more of his works.

Alyson was surprised to find herself approaching Kate's Cabins. It didn't seem possible that two hours had elapsed. She pulled into Kate's driveway, jumped out of the truck, and bounded toward the door.

Kate's smiling face greeted her. "Well, I'll be! It's little girl lost!" she shouted. "Thought maybe a grizzly got the better of you, Alyson. Come in! Come in! By the look on your face, you're filled with some sort of news you're dying to tell. It's practically bursting from you."

"Oh, Kate! It's so wonderful to see you—to hear your voice." Alyson was struck by the intensity of her feelings for this woman she'd known for such a short time. Mentally she thanked Tom Hanson for introducing her to Kate and vowed to find out more about him once she got settled. Maybe they, too, could become friends.

Kate was already busy pouring coffee and reaching

for a platter of fresh-baked blueberry muffins before Alyson had sat down.

"It seems I'm always ravenous when I see you, Kate." Alyson quickly buttered one and bit into a muffin. *My news can wait,* she thought. *This delicacy is to be savored.*

"Well," Kate pressed, obviously anxious for news, "unless you spent the past week sleeping in the great outdoors, I take it you found more than just a hunk of land when you reached your destination."

Alyson leaned back in her chair and grinned at Kate.

"Come, come, now. What have you been up to? Let's have it. Don't keep an old girl waiting," Kate said with pretended sternness.

"Kate, there's so much to tell you. I can't wait, honestly. But it wouldn't be fair to tell you now," she added mysteriously. She stared intently into her coffee cup to avoid meeting Kate's eyes.

"I assume Chad Braeburn found you after he left here in a huff?" Kate ventured after a moment.

Alyson could feel the blush beginning to spread up her face. She resolutely shifted the topic of conversation.

"I'd like to use the phone if I can, to make an appointment with a Mr. Dalton for today or tomorrow. Remember I told you I came here to see my father's property before making any decisions about it? Well, I've made my decision." Alyson was finding it very difficult to contain her excitement.

"Mr. Dalton is the lawyer for Klondike Enterprises," she continued. "My father received several letters from him on behalf of the mining company, offering to purchase his land. I couldn't understand why my father didn't want to sell, really, because the offers were more than generous. But now that I've learned some things about my father, I know why no offer would ever have been enough.''

Her eyes were shining with animation.

"I'm never going to sell the land, Kate. Never. I'm going to make an appointment to see Mr. Dalton, explain to him that the property is now mine, and tell him that I will never sell the land to Klondike Enterprises or anyone else.''

Kate looked steadily at Alyson.

"Have you told Chad already?''

"Yes, as a matter of fact, I have.'' Alyson grinned at Kate's seemingly innocent remark to trap her into revealing exactly how much she had seen of Chad.

"Then why do you have to see the lawyer? If Chad knows you aren't going to sell the land, then there's no point wasting everybody's time at Jim Dalton's.''

Alyson faltered.

"I'm not sure I understand what you're saying, Kate.'' Even as she spoke, an ominous feeling stole over her. She could feel her insides twisting in sudden anxiety.

"What I mean is, why do you have to see Jim Dalton to tell him to tell Klondike Enterprises your land is not for sale when you've already done so? It's a cockeyed way of doing things, to my thinking. Chad's the only one who makes decisions about his company. Just like his father used to do. It seems to me you've told the only person that matters.''

Alyson felt the color drain from her cheeks. She

stared dumbfounded at Kate. She put her head in her hands.

"Oh, no," she whispered. "What in heaven's name do I do now?"

Chapter Nine

"When is the next flight to Whitehorse?" Alyson enquired dully. She found it difficult to form her words. A sort of numbness had invaded her mind from the moment Kate spoke those last words. Her mind was still screaming them at her.

"Six o'clock, miss," came the perky voice of the counter clerk. "Would you like to book a seat?"

"Please," Alyson said simply. Once the transaction was accomplished, she headed outside. This time she didn't react to the crisp, fresh air. Only yesterday she would have breathed in deeply and savored the rejuvenating effect it had on her. Now she didn't care. Didn't care about anything.

Alyson walked trancelike down Main Street. She didn't attempt to acknowledge the friendly nods of passersby—couldn't and wouldn't make the effort required to conjure up a smile. Alyson welcomed the freeze that had encompassed her. It blocked the hysteria that rose up in her whenever she recalled Kate's words: "Chad's the only one who makes decisions about his company."

Her pace quickened to match the tempo of the words as they crashed about in her mind—*his company, his company.*

"Fool!" she shouted viciously, to the astonishment of the elderly gent seated peacefully on a doorstep.

How could you be so naive! she groaned inwardly. She stopped suddenly as she found herself passing the display of gold-nugget jewelry that had captured her attention the first day she arrived in Dawson. A week ago—a lifetime ago.

The magic and the mystery of this place is real, she thought. *But dreams don't come true. Silly dreams. Silly Alyson Langdon.*

The tears that she had managed to hold in check sprang forth at last. The large gold nugget in the window was replaced by an image of Chad, staring at her with that ridiculous lopsided grin on his face, a gold nugget resting against his chest. She fled toward the river.

The fierce current of the river matched the fierceness she felt coursing through her veins. Her tears were replaced by anger—anger aimed directly at herself.

Flashes of conversations—conversations that now made sense to her—flitted through her mind. "I want it all," Chad had said. "The land. The mine. Love and passion."

Yes, she realized, his eyes lit up with bold passion

whenever he had spoken about the land and his mine—
unashamed to speak of the love he felt. But never once
had he said he loved *her*.

"You're the most wonderful thing that has ever happened to me," he had murmured as he'd held her in
his arms. And, "Here's to us and the wonderful relationship ahead," he had said, clinking his glass
against hers.

*But never love. He never said he loved me. He only
spoke of a future relationship.*

Alyson sat down quickly as the realization of what
had happened struck her. That she loved him was not
in question. She knew with every fiber of her being
that she loved Chad Braeburn more than she could
describe in words. Many times during the week he had
attempted to bring up the subject of business. Every
time she had prevented him from doing so. Chad had
intended to tell her that he was the owner of Klondike
Enterprises. She knew he did. She had to believe he
did.

*But does he love me? Does he truly know that he
loves me?* she asked herself. *I'll never know because
of the stupid land!*

Questions kept bombarding her. *Was I just trying to
live out Dad's dream? Did the ghosts of the past invade
my way of thinking, my emotions? Sorry, Dad, but I
can't live out your dreams. You didn't take a chance—
instead decided to play it safe. You ended up losing.
Well, I'm going to make very sure it's Alyson Langdon
that he wants—just Alyson Langdon.*

At once, with great clarity, she understood the only
course of action she could, and would, take. The ghosts

would be put to rest, and she would assume control of her own destiny, she vowed.

She strode down Main Street with a sense of purpose. She stared at the sign on the door—DALTON & DALTON. With an air of determination, she opened the door and stepped in.

"If you will just sign here, Miss Langdon."

Jim Dalton pushed the agreement toward Alyson and offered her his pen. He watched the young lady seated in front of him hesitate for a moment before taking a deep breath and signing her name to the document that transferred ownership of the Langdon property to Klondike Enterprises.

"I'm sure you won't regret the decision," he said kindly. "The offer is extremely generous."

Alyson looked at him with a strangely sad smile on her face.

"Yes, it is. It would seem that no price is too high. My visit here has made me realize just how desperately Klondike Enterprises wants the land. Your ready acceptance of my offer to sell at twice the previously suggested price has convinced me my instincts were right."

She looked once more at the document in front of her, then with a determined air returned the papers and the pen.

"Thank you, Mr. Dalton, for agreeing to arrange for the effects from the cabin to be shipped to me in San Francisco. I have booked a flight to leave Dawson tonight. I want to make sure there is nothing else that remains to be done."

Jim tore off a copy of the purchase agreement and folded it carefully before passing it across the desk to Alyson.

"That's everything, Miss Langdon. The check for two hundred thousand dollars will be in your bank account by the time you get back home." He stood up and offered Alyson his hand. "I'm very sorry about your father."

Alyson took the extended hand numbly. "Thank you," she murmured.

The door closed behind her as she stepped out onto Main Street.

Jim Dalton rubbed his hands in triumph.

"What time is Chad Braeburn coming in, Sally?"

"Four o'clock, he said." She eyed her boss curiously. "Why are you so excited?"

"Because, my dear girl, that young lady who just walked out of here has just sold Harry Langdon's property to Klondike Enterprises. Signed, sealed, and delivered. Our esteemed Mr. Braeburn has been foaming at the mouth about that land for the last two years. Then in walks Harry Langdon's daughter out of the blue, informs me that the land is now hers, and offers to sell it immediately." He stopped rubbing his hands for a moment. "She's a cool customer. Gave me an ultimatum—double the price or no go. No discussion. No consultation. Take it or leave it." He stroked his chin contemplatively. "Fortunately, Chad had authorized me to make repeated offers to Harry Langdon up to two hundred fifty thousand dollars maximum."

Sally raised her eyebrows. "That's quite a price for that piece of property."

"Well, Chad wants it pretty badly. The rest of the land isn't of much value if he can't get access to it. I think he's going to be pleasantly surprised when he gets here. Indeed I do!"

He returned to his office, whistling cheerfully.

It was exactly four o'clock when Chad pulled up in front of Jim Dalton's office.

"Afternoon, Sally," he called out confidently as he strode by her desk. "Jim's expecting me, I trust?"

"Go right in, Chad," Sally said lamely to his back as he opened the door to Jim's office, not waiting for her reply.

Chad reached out to shake Jim's extended hand.

"Well, you're certainly riding on cloud nine," Jim boomed. "Did Sally already give you the good news?"

"I didn't stop long enough to hear Sally's good news, Jim." Chad laughed. "What happened? Did she finally get that raise she's been harping about for the past three years?" he teased.

"Easy, easy, Chad. Don't let the gal hear you. You know perfectly well I gave Sally a generous raise some months ago," Jim replied, clearly flustered at Chad's ribbing. "Come in. I've got some news for you," he said, ushering him inside his office.

"This must be your lucky day," he continued. "You look like the cat that swallowed the canary, from that self-satisfied look on your face. How're you doing?"

"Pretty well, thanks, Jim. If you don't mind, I'd like you to look over this contract before you give me your news. I want Sally to have it typed and ready for signature by five o'clock."

Chad handed a single sheet of paper to Jim and

settled himself comfortably in a chair. It was difficult to control the grin playing on his lips. Jim Dalton wasn't going to be expecting this. That was for sure.

He watched as Jim's eyes ran down the points he had outlined. For a moment the lawyer stopped reading; then his eyes flicked back to the beginning of the page and started again. He put the paper down on the desk and took off his glasses.

"What the devil is going on here?"

"I'm giving land to Alyson Langdon as a—"

"I can read that," Jim interrupted abruptly. "But what are you doing, Chad? I've just spent two hundred thousand dollars of yours purchasing the Harry Langdon property. I have the document right here in front of me."

"What!"

"This document is a bill of sale. Alyson Langdon was here two hours ago. I accepted her offer on your behalf."

Chad jumped to his feet and snatched the papers off Jim's desk. A look of total disbelief crossed his face.

He feasted his eyes on the document, turning it over in his hands in search of . . . what? Evidence of its validity? All blood drained from his face, and his hands shook in fury.

"Now," he said ominously, "give it to me, Jim. What's this all about? Tell me what happened. What did she say?"

Jim stared into Chad's eyes in an effort to fathom what was happening. He shrugged in resignation and offered the details.

"Alyson Langdon showed up here a few hours ago

armed with documents that proved her rightful owner of the land. Harry died a few months ago—that's obviously why we didn't get a response to that latest offer. Did you know that, Chad?''

''Just go on'' was Chad's blunt reply.

''She said she was willing to sell the land at double the last offer.''

''Just that?'' Chad interjected rudely. ''Did she give a reason? Come on, Jim, I want to know her exact words.''

Clearly puzzled by Chad's behavior, Jim continued, this time with a hint of anger in his voice.

''She said, 'I have no need for this land, no love of this land. Just let me sign the papers, and I'll be on my way back to San Francisco—where I belong.' ''

''Two hundred thousand dollars? You offered her that much?'' The disbelief in Chad's voice was mirrored by the look of absolute astonishment on his face.

Jim straightened his shoulders and nervously adjusted his tie. ''I didn't offer her anything, Chad. She came here this afternoon and said she would sell the land to Klondike Enterprises for twice the amount of money we had offered her father. She gave me precisely five seconds to make up my mind. Since I had your approval for an offer up to two hundred fifty thousand, I didn't hesitate. It was all done in less than ten minutes.''

Chad sat back down in the chair abruptly. His lips tightened into a thin, straight line. ''So, she sold out. The first opportunity came along, and she sold out. 'I'll never sell this land, never.' And I believed it!''

The bewilderment on Jim's face seemed to fuel a

rising anger in Chad. "What else did she say? Come on, Jim, what did she say?"

The color had returned to Chad's face, and the pallor of a moment ago was replaced by a vivid, angry red. His dark eyes smoldered as they fixed themselves on Jim.

"Chad, I'm sorry. I thought you'd be delighted. I. . . . She said something about following her instincts. That she thought she'd get double the price offered her father. That Klondike Enterprises would be responsible for packing all the belongings in the cabin and shipping them to San Francisco. And that she was leaving Dawson tonight on the evening plane."

"Anything else?" Chad asked coldly.

"Except that I promised her the money would be in her bank account by the time she got back to San Francisco," Jim finished lamely. "I'm sorry—"

"Forget it. It has nothing to do with you," Chad cut in curtly. "I wanted the land, and I got it." He stood up and took the contract he had drawn up from Jim's hand. "I was the one who authorized you to pay up to two hundred fifty thousand. There's nothing for you to be sorry for. I might as well take my copy of the purchase agreement with me."

At the door he hesitated for a moment before turning back to Jim. "I trust you'll continue to respect a client's confidentiality. If ever a hint of what I had written ever reaches my ears, I'll know exactly where the information came from. Do I make myself clear?"

"Certainly."

"I'll take care of the arrangements for shipping Miss

Langdon's effects out of here. It will give me a great deal of pleasure.''

He turned abruptly on his heel and strode out of the room. Jim heard the front door of the building slam behind him.

Chad fought hard to control his fury. He jumped into his truck and sped toward Kate's, spraying gravel as he cranked the truck into gear. He couldn't think clearly. His mind was filled only with the words Alyson said to Jim.

A quick check of Cabin 3 proved that Alyson and her belongings were gone. Chad knocked boldly on Kate's door.

''Chad,'' Kate spoke hurriedly. ''Chad, I—''

''Is Alyson here?'' he interrupted curtly.

''Chad—''

''Answer me, Kate. Is Alyson here?'' he shouted as he attempted to look past her into the room.

''No, but—''

Chad pivoted and strode briskly toward the truck. He wouldn't hear whatever it was she had to say. With a sinking feeling, he headed toward the airport.

I don't believe it. She can't be leaving. There has to be a reasonable explanation. We made arrangements for dinner tonight. We spoke of our marriage this morning! What has gotten into her?

He spotted the truck Alyson had borrowed as soon as he reached the airport. The plane was already on the runway, and passengers were straggling toward it across the tarmac. Anxiously he scanned the group. No Alyson. He ran to the terminal building. A few people were still hanging around, waving their last farewells through the windows. The flight attendants in charge of tickets were checking the final lists, and the last call announcement was blaring out.

Chad rushed to the counter.

"Alyson Langdon. Is there an Alyson Langdon on this flight?"

"Mr. Braeburn, we can't—"

"This is an emergency. Is Alyson Langdon on this flight?"

The clerk hesitated a moment before pulling up a list of passengers on her computer screen.

"Langdon. Langdon. Yes, there is a Miss Langdon . . . Mr. Braeburn, you can't go through security. Stop! Mr. Braeburn!"

Chad was already through the gate and on the runway before her sentence was finished.

At the entrance to the plane, he spotted Alyson three rows down. He roughly pushed aside the steward who tried to restrain him and strode down the aisle. He stopped beside Alyson's seat, arms crossed in front of him, legs braced as if ready to do battle. This time there was only menace in his lopsided grin. The cold, black eyes flashed with recrimination. It was apparent he was struggling for control: Every muscle in his body was flexed; his menacing grin turned into a cynical sneer.

"So, you got your price, Cheechako," Chad snarled vehemently. "Now, go back to the city. Go back where you belong."

The startled passengers stopped their chatter and turned to stare at this man who shouted with such venom at the young woman in the green linen suit and champagne silk blouse.

"It's all right. I've said my piece," Chad thundered at the steward, who was calling for assistance on the radio phone. "I'm leaving." And he pushed his way past the few remaining passengers who still waited on the steps outside.

He stared beyond the small crowd gathering to see what the commotion was all about. There'd be talk in town, but he didn't care. There was talk when Norah left him; let them talk all they wanted now. He'd made a fool of himself, and he was beyond caring.

The plane took off just as he was approaching his truck. He felt his heart lurch, but he refused to turn round or to look up. He kicked the truck Alyson had been using as he passed by and then slammed his own door shut and started the engine.

The next few weeks blurred into an endless series of meetings, contracts, and negotiations. Chad worked and slept. When he remembered, he ate. Whenever the thought of Alyson entered his mind, he picked up the phone and scheduled another meeting to speed up the expansion of the mine. A road had been bulldozed on the outer edge of the property that had belonged to Harry Langdon, and men were already at work on the land to the north. The cabin remained where it was.

"I said I wanted the road at the edge, and that's where the road goes," had been his surly answer when one of the developers pointed out that it would be more efficient to run it directly through the property.

Chad had been at the cabin the day the packers

arrived. He watched moodily from a slouched position in the doorway. Alyson had obviously had no time to pack. The only things she seemed to have taken were her father's diaries. The sweatshirt with teddy bears on it was draped over the sofa alongside one of his own sweaters. He picked them both up.

Kate had been asking about him, one of his men told him. He didn't go to see her. He didn't go to town. He slept in his office. When he woke up in a sweat in the middle of the night with the image of auburn hair tumbling over Alyson's shoulders, he sat at his desk and reworked the plans made the day before. He had wanted the land, and he had gotten it. He determined to work it with a vengeance.

The night finally came when the image dancing in front of him refused to submit to the mounds of paper on the desk. Chad stared at the top sheet with the single word *Alyson* written on it over and over. He laid down his pen and put his head in his hands.

"Why couldn't you tell me to my face that you'd changed your mind? It would have hurt, but it would have been better than sneaking off behind my back." Chad said the words out loud. At least he would never have shouted at her so shamefully in front of a group of strangers. He might have been able to change her mind. For the first time in six weeks, he allowed himself to think about Alyson.

The money had been deposited into her account. He wondered what she had decided to do with it. Never once when she had talked to him had she talked about dreams of being rich, what she would do if she had all the money she wanted. Money hadn't seemed all that important to her. Why, then, had she demanded such an outrageous price? *Why? Why? Why?* pounded in his head until it ached.

He got up and went to the bathroom for a glass of water and aspirin. He looked at himself in the mirror. His face was lined from lack of sleep; the eyes that stared back were tired and lifeless. He realized with a bit of a shock that he must have forgotten to shave; the stubble on his chin reflected more than overnight growth.

Pull yourself together, Braeburn, he told himself sternly. *You wanted the land, and you've got it.* The eyes continued to stare back dully. *But I want Alyson more!*

He gulped down the aspirin, set the glass roughly on the counter, and went back to his desk. He picked up the piece of paper with Alyson's name scrawled every which way on it. Even the sight of the name set his blood pounding.

She must have found out I owned the land. If Jim didn't tell her, then Kate must have. She must have gone to Kate's first.

Chad closed his eyes and tried to feel how Alyson must have reacted at the news. She'd have been shocked, of course. And confused. She'd promised to marry a man who over the week had shared her most intimate thoughts. But he hadn't told her what everyone else in Dawson City knew. She must have felt duped, to say the least. Chad could understand how upset and used she must have felt—and angry. He would have been tempted to simply take off under the same circumstances. What puzzled him, however, was the decision to sell the land. Not only to sell it, but to demand double the amount of the offer.

It didn't make sense.

If she still didn't know that he owned Klondike Enterprises, then she must have gotten cold feet about marriage. She'd changed her mind and didn't have the courage to tell him in person. But then why would she have sold the land? Would she have given up her father's dream just because she would feel too embarrassed to return to the Yukon? It was possible. But it still didn't make sense.

Norah had never disguised her desire to get back to the city and the fast lane. Chad hadn't gone seeking her when she left, because he knew there was no changing her mind. But Alyson wasn't Norah. And he was not the Chad he once had been.

I let her go, though, he told himself wearily. *I even gave her a great send-off. I made it clear I never wanted her back here. So what is there left to do now?*

He picked up the phone.

"I'm sorry, Kate. I know it's some ungodly hour. I have to talk to you. . . . Yes, it is important. It's terribly important. . . . Thanks. I'm on my way. Bless you, Kate."

It was five o'clock in the morning when a bleary-eyed Kate opened the door.

"I was wondering when you'd come to your senses," she said simply.

Chapter Ten

"Are you sure you don't mind?"

Alyson shook her head and smiled at Janet's obvious delight.

"I honestly don't mind. I don't have any plans for the weekend, so I might as well work."

"You're an angel, Alyson. I owe you one." Janet flashed one last grateful smile, then disappeared through the staff-room door before Alyson had a chance to change her mind.

Alyson finished the last of her sandwich and checked the time. There was still a quarter of an hour left before she was back on duty. She picked up one of the magazines on the coffee table and flicked through the pages, but found nothing of interest. It was still the vacation season, and much of the advertising attempted to lure visitors to far-off lands with exotic beaches.

Being back at work is like a vacation in comparison to the last few weeks, she thought. *The last thing I need is another vacation.*

The door opened, and Janet popped her head back in.

"Want to go shopping with me after work today? There's a good sale on at À la Mode, and I'd like to get something spiffy to wear for my date on Saturday. You know, something really special."

Alyson hesitated. The thought of helping her friend select some romantic outfit to impress the latest love in her life held no appeal, but she didn't want to spoil Janet's euphoria.

"Come on," Janet insisted. "We haven't been anywhere together since you got back from the Yukon. I know you're hiding something. I can tell." Her eyes glinted with curiosity. "But I promise not to pry if you'll let me tell you about this gorgeous guy I met in my night-school class. We can go for a bite to eat after. I'm dying to tell somebody."

"Okay," Alyson submitted with a forced smile. "But no heart-to-heart."

Janet pursed her lips as she surveyed her friend from the doorway. There was no getting past Alyson when she had that stubborn look on her face. *She'll come 'round in time,* she thought. *But she sure didn't like something about that vacation.*

In the end Janet settled on a blue silk dress that draped flatteringly over her slender figure.

"You don't think the black one would have looked more sophisticated?" she asked Alyson anxiously as they munched on a Caesar salad.

Alyson blushed guiltily at her friend's sudden wavering. In fact, the black dress had looked stunning, but the reminder had been too painful for her.

"You look lovely in the blue. Black can be too dressy. You'll be able to wear this one to far more things," she managed to say truthfully. "Anyway, the price of the black dress was outrageous."

"Tell me about it," Janet groaned. "I've already spent next week's pay as it is. Oh, to be independently wealthy!" she sighed.

Alyson thought of the two hundred thousand dollars sitting in her bank account. She hadn't checked, but she assumed it was there. Once back in San Francisco, she had tried to pick up her life where she had left off, budgeting her meager pay to cover the bills and setting a little aside for a splurge sometime. The thought of using some of the money from Chad repelled her.

"You've been pushing that piece of lettuce around for the last five minutes," Janet said meaningfully. "What's gotten into you lately?"

"Nothing. I'm just not hungry, I guess." Alyson looked disconsolately at her plate. She poked once more at the salad and then set her fork down and pushed the plate aside.

"I really should get going, Jan. My place is a mess, and I made a firm promise to myself that I would spend tonight catching up on all the housework I've been putting off. The dress looks gorgeous. Really it does." She smiled apologetically at her friend, who nodded in resignation.

"I know. I know," she grumbled, joining Alyson at the checkout. "You'll tell me later. It's the story of my life. I'm blessed with an inordinate amount of curiosity that no one wants to satisfy until later.''

Alyson couldn't help laughing at the woebegone expression on her face. She gave Janet's arm a quick squeeze.

''At least you have someone to occupy your mind for the rest of the evening,'' she teased. ''Come on. There's a bus in five minutes.''

Alyson waved good-bye and stepped out into the evening air. It was hot and sultry. Even in the light cotton dress she was wearing, she felt oppressed by the heavy heat. Irritably she brushed a strand of hair off her forehead. A lady pushed past her on the sidewalk, her parcels bumping against her. Rush hour on Powell Street never used to bother her, but today she felt hemmed in by the people pushing their way through the crowds, intent only on getting to their destination. The wailing siren of an ambulance urgently clearing a path through the snarled traffic grated on her ears.

The bus was packed with commuters. She joined the other passengers, who were already standing tightly wedged against each other. At the corner of Powell and 6th she struggled out of the line and stepped off the bus.

''I'm going crazy in this place,'' she muttered to herself. ''If I see any more people or hear any more noise today, I'll scream!''

The telephone was ringing when Alyson reached the door of her apartment. *Chad* was the first name that flashed to her mind. She unlocked the door hurriedly and dashed to the kitchen. The ringing stopped before she got there. A dull dial tone was the only answer to her excited "Hello." Angrily she kicked off her shoes and flopped onto the sofa. Darn Janet! If she'd just come home as she had wanted to do in the first place, she'd have been in when the phone rang.

Get over him, Alyson, she admonished herself. *He's not going to call. He got what he really wanted. If he'd wanted you, he'd have stopped you from leaving in the first place, you fool.*

Even now she flinched at the scene on the plane—those dark eyes full of anger, the coldness in his accusation. *"Go home, Cheechako. Go back where you belong."* The words had mortified her. Everyone on the plane had heard him. They all knew who he was, and they'd stared at her in horrified fascination. The ride to Vancouver had been the most humiliating experience of her life.

Many times since her return she had picked up the phone to make contact with Chad. The first thing she did when she got back was to call directory assistance to find out his telephone number. She knew it by heart: She had dialed it at least three times a week. Once she even let it ring four times before she hung up. She longed to hear his voice, but she couldn't be the one to make contact. If she did, she might as well have saved herself all this heartache and simply stayed and married him in the first place.

I wish I had, she sighed. *Sometimes I wish I had. But I would always have wondered if he'd married me to get the land. The doubt would have eaten away at me and eventually destroyed us, I know it.*

She looked at her father's diaries neatly stacked in the corner of the living room. She had brought them back herself on the plane, fearful of their safety. However, she hadn't opened them since her return. Everything else from the cabin had arrived two weeks ago. It was impossible to fit anything more in the small apartment, so she had put the furniture in storage. Most of the clothes she had taken on vacation were among the cartons at home, but she couldn't bring herself to look at them. She left them unopened.

The letter she had started to Kate two weeks ago lay unfinished on the coffee table. She picked it up and read what she had written. There was nothing in it about Chad—just a thank-you for her kindness and general chit-chat about the weather and the home. *Sincerely, Alyson,* she scrawled across the bottom, folded the letter neatly, and sealed it in the envelope. She hoped Kate would understand.

"What are you doing here today? I thought this was your weekend off." The question was fired in a rather indignant way. Mrs. Parsons liked to be on top of things. It wasn't right when people went and changed things on you and got you all confused.

"Oh, Janet had lots of interesting things to do," Alyson replied in a conciliatory tone. "So I swapped with her."

"Another new boyfriend, I suppose." Mrs. Parsons sniffed in a disapproving way. "When I was young, we weren't allowed to go out with any Tom, Dick, or Harry. We had to have our parents' approval." She twisted her hands, gnarled from rheumatism, agitatedly in her lap.

Alyson sat down beside her. They were in the TV

room that for once was quiet. A bingo game in the cafeteria accounted for the unusual emptiness.

"Didn't you want to play bingo today?" Alyson asked. Mrs. Parsons was beginning to worry her. Usually she was one of the strongest supports in the nursing home, involved in whatever activity might be going on, impatient when Alyson and her coworkers tried to do too much for her. "I'm not an imbecile yet, you know," was the reproach most of them received.

For the past week the old lady seemed to have lost interest in what was going on around her. Much to Alyson's astonishment, she had irritably complained this morning that no one ever offered to help her. Alyson had written down her concerns in the log book that the supervisor would go through that night.

"I'm too old to play bingo. I can't hold the pen, and I feel stupid having someone else mark the numbers for me. Besides, most of them cheat."

Alyson sighed. Usually she had more time on weekends to catch up on paperwork while her charges spent time with their families, who visited or played bingo with the less fortunate in the cafeteria. Mrs. Parsons was going to be ornery today.

"What's this boyfriend like, anyway?"

Instantly Alyson thought of Chad. A smile lit up her face before she realized her mistake.

"I haven't met him. I'm sure he's very nice. Janet hasn't stopped talking about him all week, and she spent hours on Tuesday looking for a dress to wear tonight."

"Umph."

"Would you like to go outside for a little walk? It's

a lovely day. A bit of fresh air will do us both good. I can catch up on my reports later.''

Mrs. Parsons didn't refuse Alyson's help getting into the wheelchair. Her thin hand clutched her arm tightly as she allowed herself to be guided onto the seat. *She's so frail,* Alyson realized with alarm.

"It doesn't make any difference, you know," Mrs. Parsons said unexpectedly as Alyson pushed the wheelchair along the path to the garden behind the home.

"What doesn't?"

"What you do with your life."

Alyson didn't reply. She knew Mrs. Parsons would get around to saying what she wanted to say in her own good time. They stopped beside a garden bench set in a sheltered corner of the garden. Alyson put the brakes on the wheelchair, adjusted the blanket tucked around Mrs. Parsons, and sat down on the bench.

"All you do in the end is die, anyway," the old lady continued, looking straight ahead of her. "Once they've got you stashed away, nobody thinks of you anymore."

"That's not true," Alyson replied gently. "You shouldn't talk that way."

"Umph. I'd like to hear what you have to say when you get to be an old, useless woman like me—no good to anybody, least of all herself." Mrs. Parsons's lower lip began to quiver. With a determined effort to stop the tears from coming, she lifted her chin defiantly and looked at Alyson. The proud gesture didn't disguise the fear in the soft brown eyes.

Alyson took the gnarled hand in hers. "You're not useless to me," she consoled. "Nobody's useless. Do you know how often I thought of you and talked about you all while I was away? I missed you very much. And I saw a beautiful quilt in that log-cabin pattern you love so much. I thought of you as soon as I set eyes on it.''

''You're a nice girl.'' The trembling was gone from the voice. ''But I think I'd like to go back in now. I'm tired today.''

Mrs. Parsons didn't join the others for supper. When Alyson went to check on her, she was sleeping in her room. Her breathing was slow and labored.

''I'm phoning the doctor,'' Alyson told Rena, who was sharing the shift with her. ''I'm not waiting for the supervisor.''

''Alyson, you're a very good nurse. I understand how you feel, but you know that you can't allow yourself to get too emotionally involved.'' The supervisor, Mrs. Byrd, looked at the young woman standing in front of her desk. *She looks tired,* she mused, *but that doesn't entirely account for that serious expression.* Although always eager to please, there was a stubborn streak in Alyson that emerged from time to time. She had seen it before—jaw set, lips firm, eyes steady and unwavering. The main giveaway, however, was the voice. When Alyson asked in that very quiet, deliberate, measured tone if she could go with Mrs. Parsons to the hospital, Mrs. Byrd knew she would be hard to dissuade.

Better now than have her go after a full ten-hour shift, she thought. *And I have the distinct feeling that that is exactly what she will do.*

"The nurses there will look after her very well. You know that," she tried persuasively. "How would you feel if another nurse came in here to keep an eye on someone because they felt they might not be getting the best care in the world?"

"I'd be glad," Alyson flashed back. "Anyway, it's better to come here than to go to the hospital. Mrs. Parsons is frightened. I could see the fear in her eyes today. Her relatives won't make it here for a couple of days. I'll come straight back here, I promise. I just want her to be with someone she knows on the way there."

"And after your shift is over?" It was none of Mrs. Byrd's business, and she knew it. But it was worth a try.

Alyson didn't reply. Her lips tightened, and her gaze remained steady as she looked at Mrs. Byrd without saying a word.

"All right, all right." Mrs. Byrd sighed. "And I'm sure we can manage without you for the last three hours of your shift. If not, I know where to get ahold of you." She saw Alyson's face relax. But there was no gloating in the half smile. "Just make sure you go home later and get a good night's sleep," she added gruffly. She noted the lack of comment. "If you go on like this, you're going to end up in the psychiatric ward, and then where would we be?"

Alyson waited patiently for Mrs. Byrd to finish. She knew her well enough to let her continue without interruption. If she started to argue, she might change her mind about letting her go. And she knew Mrs. Byrd was right. She was too involved with her charges, all of them, but she had a particularly soft spot for Mrs. Parsons, and the sudden decline in her health had thrown her into a panic.

She had felt her throat constrict and her heart pound when the doctor had suggested Mrs. Parsons be sent to the hospital immediately. She wanted to scream at him, hit him for talking in such a sensible, matter-of-fact way. Her throat was so tight that she found it difficult to formulate words. "I'll tell Mrs. Byrd right away," she had managed to say in what she hoped sounded like a very sensible, matter-of-fact voice.

The evening was long. Mrs. Parsons slept most of the time, aided by a sedative and antibiotics intended to stave off the pneumonia that threatened to set in.

"Is she a relative of yours?" the young nurse asked sympathetically.

"Yes," Alyson replied. "Sort of." The nurse didn't hear the added comment as she concentrated on changing the medication dripping through the intravenous. She nodded only in an abstract way and left the two of them to tend to the next patient.

Mrs. Parsons is about as much family as I've got, Alyson thought. *I've got no father. No mother. No husband to go home to or worry about. No children. My career is my family.*

"Would you call me if Mrs. Parsons gets worse during the night?" Alyson asked the staff nurse on duty. It was already midnight, but Alyson had managed to hang around the hospital. In her own nurse's uniform, she had looked as though she belonged to the place and hadn't volunteered to change anyone's impression of the truth. "Her daughters have been contacted, but neither of them can get here for a couple of days. I promised them I would act as their stand-in until they arrived.'' Mrs. Byrd had telephoned the relatives, but Alyson felt no guilt in the lie.

''We'll call if it's serious. But I'm sure she's going to be all right. Go home and get some rest.''

''Home.'' The word had a hollow ring to it. She hailed a taxi.

At four o'clock she was startled out of a deep sleep. *It can't be time to get up to work already,* she groaned, reaching for the alarm clock. She tried desperately to focus her eyes on the time, then realized it was the insistent ringing of the phone that had jolted her awake. Chad? At four o'clock in the morning? Without bothering to grab her housecoat or slippers, she ran to the kitchen.

''Hello,'' she said, excitement welling up within her.

''This is St. Mary's Hospital. Could I speak to Miss Landgon, please?''

Alyson awoke in alarm, her mouth poised for a scream.

It was one of many nightmares that had wrenched her from sleep over the past two weeks. At first she had been frightened by the demons that invaded her nights; now she was just dreadfully frustrated.

She could never recall the specifics of the dreams. She only knew that the events that gave them life always took place in the wilderness, always centered around Chad and Mrs. Parsons.

Alyson leaped out of bed and wandered to the kitchen

to pour herself a glass of milk. She slumped into an easy chair and stared out the window at the lights of San Francisco.

"Well, at least I got used to you again, San Francisco," she said aloud.

For the first two weeks after her return, her nights had been spent tossing and turning. City sounds had pierced her sleep. She had longed for the stillness of a Yukon night and Chad's arms around her.

Stay out of my dreams, Chad, she thought. *Stay in the Yukon where you belong—with your almighty land.*

He left her alone during the day. But at night, while she was sleeping, he waltzed into her subconscious and paid a visit—at night, when she let down the shield she had erected around her heart. She had to cope somehow.

Curled up in the easy chair, she thought over recent events. The last six weeks had drained her. For the first few days after her return from the Yukon, she neither ate nor slept. She had holed up in her apartment, alternating between staring vacantly at the walls and pacing. She hadn't had the energy or the inclination to cry. Emptiness—just emptiness had tormented her.

It wasn't until five days had passed that she had made an effort to pull herself out of her lethargy. After all, she had to face the world sooner or later.

She was horrified by the image that greeted her when she took her first real look at herself in the mirror. It had taken a full minute to realize who the bedraggled-looking creature staring back at her was. Alyson was shocked—and disconcerted—by her appearance: black circles ringing glazed, dull eyes; hair hanging limp, without the slightest sign of vitality; sheer desperation etched on her charcoal-tinged skin.

After much preparation, a resemblance of her old physical self emerged. She accepted the fact that it might take a bit longer to repair the damage to her emotional self, but she vowed then and there to do so.

It was a harder task than she had imagined.

Returning to work had been the easiest—and hardest—part. Getting back into a routine that was familiar was easy. Facing her charges and their rampant curiosity and enthusiasm about her vacation was not.

Even Mrs. Parsons's death couldn't stop Grampa Hill from bombarding her with endless questions. She wondered if he and the others would ever tire of their preoccupation with her life. Because it was expected, Alyson regaled them with tales of her activities—most of which held an element of truth. She did not, however, inform them that she had already been in town a week before returning to work.

Grampa Hill still continued to tease her unmercifully. She was proud that she was able to abide his playful teasing without screaming.

"Why, the men up there must be starved for a pretty little thing like you," he prodded and snooped. "You can't fool me, Miss Langdon. How many hearts did you break?"

"I assure you, none," she replied lightheartedly. *Except my own,* she added to herself. "The men of the Yukon are far too serious about their search for gold to be devastated by my charm, Mr. Hill."

"Well, seems to me the trip must have plum tuckered you out," he persisted. "You look exhausted, girl.

Dark circles beneath those lovely green eyes, twitchy as all get-out, and preoccupied, you're always preoccupied. Why, just yesterday, you brought me apple juice when I clearly requested orange juice. And you know how I can't abide apple juice. The nurse that replaced you was always muddling up my orders and. . . ."

Alyson breathed a sigh of relief when, as usual, he lost sight of his main topic, instead focusing on the minor, yet more important, events of his life.

"Bless your sweet, uncomplicated heart, Mr. Hill," Alyson murmured now as she rose from her easy chair and headed back to bed. She willed herself to fall asleep.

The next morning Alyson stood under the nozzle of the shower for an extra five minutes in a vain attempt to draw more energy from the pounding water. *One more day of work, then two glorious days off,* she thought. *I can make it.*

This time I'll get more rest—I'm talking to you, Chad Braeburn—and make better use of my time, she thought while turning off the taps. *And maybe I'll accept that dinner invitation, after all. As long as my charming doctor friend doesn't suggest a picnic.* This time her lips turned into a wistful smile as the thought of teddy bears breezed by.

There was more spring in Alyson's step as she emerged from the bedroom wearing a crisp, white uniform. Her hair was knotted in a single braid falling over her shoulder. Images of another time, not very long ago, when she wore her hair this way filtered into her mind. She quickly banished the memories and set off to the kitchen.

She sat at the kitchen table, ready to tackle her hearty breakfast of bacon and eggs. Glancing toward the living room, she forced her gaze to rest on the boxes that were piled in one corner. They'd been stacked there for four weeks. Until now she had refused to acknowledge their intrusion in the room. Chad had certainly wasted no time shipping her belongings from the cabin. It hurt her to think that he could cut her out of his life so quickly.

How could I have been so very, very mistaken? she wondered.

She knew that she had been taking a gamble when she threw the land back in his face. But she had never doubted that it was the only thing to do. She had grossly misjudged his reaction.

She had spotted him from the moment he burst out of the terminal doors onto the tarmac. Instantly her heart had exploded with joy. He was coming after her to stop her from leaving! It had worked! She'd won!

When Alyson caught sight of the look of fury in his smoldering black eyes as he pushed his way past startled passengers and attendants, the joy turned to despair.

You had no right to test him, she thought, still staring at the boxes. *It was stupid to gamble, stupid to set the stakes so high. You knew how proud he was, how passionate he was about everything—especially the land.*

She rose and scraped the remainder of her breakfast from her plate. She'd hardly touched a thing, as usual.

He doesn't love you! Get that into your head! She flung the plate into the sink with no regard for its fragility.

Tonight, she thought, *I will come home and immediately go through the contents of those offensive cartons.* She grabbed her coat and purse and headed off to work, thankful to get away from the objects that taunted her so.

"Morning, folks," she cheerfully greeted the patients seated in the TV room, already arguing about what to watch next.

She knew she'd ultimately be the one to decide. They expected that of her and never held a grudge when she made her pronouncements. It was easy. Alyson knew what each of them wanted to watch and merely rotated her choices. Each of them won, so to speak, at some point during the day.

Alyson sat down at her desk, intending to review the charts from the night shift and to scan the activities scheduled for today. Instead, she opened her desk drawer and located the phone number Jason Michaels had given her. She smiled as she picked up the phone and dialed his number.

"Good morning. Dr. Michaels's office," came the officious voice of the receptionist.

"Hello. This is Alyson Langdon," she replied smoothly. "May I speak to him, please?"

"Dr. Michaels is with a patient at the moment," the receptionist replied automatically. "May I help you?"

"I'm afraid not. It's personal. Perhaps you could

ask him to call me when he's free." There was a hint of coolness in Alyson's response.

"Oh," came the reply, wavering with uncertainty. "If you'll just leave your number, I'll—"

"Thank you. That won't be necessary. He has my number," Alyson interrupted, hanging up, feeling just a touch spiteful. She never really cared for Jason Michaels's stolid employee.

It took exactly three minutes for Jason to return her call. Alyson deliberately waited until the fourth ring before answering.

"Alyson. How wonderful to hear from you!" Jason said, clearly pleased that she had contacted him. "I had just about given up hope that you would get back to me!" There was subtle admonishment in his voice.

Alyson couldn't help comparing even that small flaw in Jason's personality to Chad's. There was nothing subtle about Chad. He said what he meant, to your face, in front of anybody and everybody. She pushed further thoughts of Chad Braeburn from her mind.

"Well, Jason," Alyson said with a laugh, "I am free this evening after all and would love to accept that dinner invitation. If I haven't left it too late, that is."

"Wonderful," Jason responded enthusiastically. "And no, of course it isn't too late. Would seven o'clock be okay?"

"Seven is fine," she replied calmly. "See you then."

She sighed as she replaced the receiver. "Picnic time for teddy bears" were the only words that came to mind.

* * *

Alyson had dressed with special care that evening. She wore her hair swept back into a demure knot at her nape. Her dress was of white crepe de chine, simple and elegant. The black cocktail dress that she had worn with Chad at the Eldorado was pushed back into a far corner of her closet. There it would stay. Seated across from Jason in the Ports of Call dining room, she had the sensation of being a million miles away from the Eldorado, yet. . . .

"You look lovely tonight, Alyson," Jason complimented her, admiration shining from his eyes.

"Thank you, Jason. I'm sorry I took so long to accept your invitation. It's just that I've been very busy getting caught up on things at work and at home," she said, thinking that her words sounded stilted and rehearsed.

"I'm sure you've been busy," Jason responded, leaning over to replenish her glass with wine. "Tell me about your trip. I'm fascinated by the fact that you went to the Yukon. In fact, I've never known anyone who has ever gone to the Yukon. Could there really be enough there to keep a person busy for three weeks?"

There it is again, she thought. *That subtle condescension.*

"Well," she replied quickly with a smile fixed on her face, "it appears that you, like many others in the big city, believe there's nothing beyond Los Angeles and San Francisco that is really worth investigating."

Jason raised his eyebrows at her obvious rebuke.

Alyson was astonished at her backhanded insult. *You really are being rude,* she thought, *and that isn't like you. Stop punishing Jason because he isn't Chad. Jason is a very nice man. He's also a highly respected member of the medical community, good-looking in a pure, clean-cut sort of way, and so . . . proper.*

"Just teasing, Jason," Alyson added demurely. "It's just that there's a whole section of this continent that so many people don't know—and don't care— exists." Her eyes shone as she described the landscape, the stillness, the mystery of the Yukon.

"Sounds wonderful." Jason reached across the table and took her hand in his. Alyson had to stop herself from snatching her hand back. "And it seems to me that a part of you may have gotten left behind there," he said gently. "Your whole manner changes when you speak of it. Did it? Did a piece of you stay behind?"

Alyson removed her hand from his and leaned back in her chair. The questioning, unexciting face of Jason Michaels changed before her eyes. His image was replaced by the image of a man with coal-black eyes sparkling devilishly in the flicker of the candlelight, a lopsided grin reaching out to touch the very depth of her soul.

It was a long time before she found the courage to respond. When she did, there was only defeat in her breathless reply.

"Yes," Alyson said simply. "Yes. A part of me will always be there."

Chapter Eleven

The plane touched down in San Francisco.

Chad immediately unfastened his seat belt, paying no heed to the request that it remain in place until the aircraft had come to a complete stop. He was impatient to get off the plane, stretch his cramped legs, and proceed with his mission.

The flight had been comfortable enough—not too many in the first-class section, good food, plenty to drink. Nevertheless, it had been a long journey. Usually he managed to get some sleep or work on plans for the mine while he traveled. Work had been the furthest thing from his mind on this trip, and the anticipation of seeing Alyson ruled out any thought of sleep. His first thought was to book into the hotel and freshen up before he started the day. He had a lot to accomplish.

159

"Thank you for traveling with us. Have a good stay, sir."

"I sincerely hope I will." Chad smiled at the flight attendant as he stepped off the plane.

It took just under one hour for his luggage to appear on the belt and then another five minutes before he could fight his way forward to retrieve it. By the time he was able to hail a cab, he was in a rather foul mood. The cab driver aided in dispelling his bad humor by commiserating with him about the rigors of travel, especially when one landed in San Francisco.

Chad had been to San Francisco many times over the years, but not once in the last five. He was amazed by the changes that had taken place. San Francisco had boomed: The freeways were spilling over with vehicles, and construction was taking place on every piece of exposed land.

"Sorry. It's going to take longer to get down to the Sir Francis Drake Hotel," the cab driver apologized. "Morning rush hour is a zoo in San Francisco, especially on Powell Street."

Rush hour, Chad thought. *And I get annoyed when there are more than three cars ahead of me at one of the four stop signs in Dawson City.*

He pulled out his wallet and removed the slip of paper containing Alyson's address and telephone number.

"By the way, could you drive past this address on 5th Street before you take me to the hotel?" Chad requested, reaching across the seat to hand the driver the slip of paper. "You know the area?"

"Sure do. Lived here all my life," the cab driver said confidently.

Poor devil, Chad thought.

"What brings you to San Francisco, anyway? And where are you from?" the driver continued, asking the two questions he always posed to riders he picked up at the airport. He'd heard it all before but knew that customers always liked to talk about where they were from. For the first time ever, his curiosity was piqued when Chad replied that he was from the Yukon. He'd never had anyone in his cab who was from the Yukon.

"The Yukon? What's it like up there?"

"Wonderful," Chad responded with little enthusiasm in his voice. *Or at least it was,* he thought, *until Alyson left.*

"Yes, but what's it like?" the driver persisted.

Chad groaned inwardly. Good manners wouldn't allow him to ignore the question. He knew the man was truly interested in hearing about the Yukon, as most people were. Chad obliged him. At least it passed the time.

He settled back in his seat and stared indifferently at the traffic zooming by. Every time he visited a major city, it came as a shock to him that he had once been part of that life-style. The excitement he had felt as a young student was now replaced by a total disinterest.

"Here's 5th Street."

Chad sat up and scrutinized the houses as they passed. Most of them were average, middle-class homes. It was obviously not one of the wealthier areas of town. He strained to read the numbers on the houses and finally spotted an apartment block that bore the number Alyson had given.

It's certainly no great shakes, he thought. *I wonder if she's moved up in the world already. With two hundred thousand dollars, she could afford better than that.*

"I wonder what she did with the money?" he murmured.

"Who's that, sir?"

Chad turned quickly to look at the driver. Had he really spoken the words aloud? "Oh, nothing," he fumbled. "That's fine, thanks. We can be on our way now."

The cabbie stared at Chad for a moment before pulling out into the traffic.

"Do you know of any nursing homes in this area?" Chad asked once they had driven two blocks.

"Sure. A couple. One just a couple of blocks down, the other a bit farther, over on 8th. Both nice places. Hear they treat the patients real good," the driver replied with pride in his voice. "Going to visit someone?"

"Hmm," Chad grunted. *You bet I am,* he added to himself.

Twenty minutes later Chad had checked into the Sir Francis Drake Hotel. He slept for a few hours to shake the weariness from his body, then showered, shaved, and dressed. He felt his old confident self. Whenever he stayed in San Francisco on business or vacations, he always stayed at the Sir Francis Drake. The maitre d' was an old family friend, and Chad enjoyed the advantage of special treatment during his stay. Many other staff members also knew him either by name or sight. He didn't particularly admire the favoritism bestowed upon him on principle, but he was appreciative of it now. It felt good to change into neatly pressed pants and shirt, discreetly picked up and delivered during his shower.

He strode purposefully across the room and picked up the phone. There was no answer at the number Alyson had given. *Oh, well,* he thought as he put the phone back. *It's probably better to present myself at the nursing home. She can hardly throw me out of a public building, and she certainly won't throw a temper tantrum in front of her little flock.* Despite a twinge of anxiety stubbornly exerting its presence every so often, he was looking forward to the meeting.

Before he left, he looked up the addresses for the two nursing homes, deciding to visit the one on 8th Street first.

Chad paid more attention this time as the taxi sped toward the home. He noted the malls and the parks, hazarding guesses as to the likelihood of Alyson's shopping or spending time there. It was difficult for him to imagine her in the city setting. As soon as her image came into mind, he saw only the wild and unconquered land of the North.

The distance to the nursing home wasn't great; the time it took to get there was. The cab crawled through the traffic, constantly stopping and starting. Chad closed his eyes to block out the hordes of people. *How do they stand it?* he wondered. He thought of the drive from Dawson City to Hunker's Creek. *Two hours—and sometimes I never see a vehicle or a living soul.*

A perfect paradise as far as I'm concerned—or it was until Alyson left.

The cab pulled up at the front entrance.

"Visiting a relative here?" The taxi driver's voice betrayed a hint of surprise and mild disapproval that one so elegantly dressed who could afford to stay at the Sir Francis Drake Hotel should allow a relative to spend his last years in Dayton Manor.

"A friend." Chad got out of the taxi feeling slightly disgruntled at the man's curiosity and unspoken criticism. City slickers. He shrugged.

Janet spotted him as soon as he entered. Chad stood surveying the lobby with an air of ownership. Bold as brass.

"I've died and gone to heaven," Janet whispered. Her eyes swept appreciatively over Chad's body. He was dressed in a burgundy Ultrasuede sports jacket and camel-colored dress slacks, both perfectly tailored. His shirt was open at the neck, giving him a casual air.

Now, there stands the most gorgeous-looking creature I've ever laid eyes on, Janet thought, walking toward him in great anticipation.

"Hello. May I help you?" She flashed one of her brilliant smiles at him. She had to make a special effort to keep the breathlessness out of her voice.

He looked at the pretty young woman and hoped that he had chosen the right nursing home.

"I'm looking for Alyson Langdon." He smiled, staring boldly into Janet's eyes, willing her to give the correct response.

"Oh," Janet replied simply, feeling disappointment wash over her. "Alyson Langdon. You must be Dr.

Michaels.'' *Now I know why Alyson kept this one to herself,* she thought jealously.

"Dr. Michaels sounds awfully formal.'' Chad grinned to hide the pang of anger that stabbed at him.

Don't be so mean, Janet chastised herself. *Alyson deserves some happiness. She's been through the wringer these past few months.* Janet's natural friendliness and charm emerged as she responded, "Sorry, Jason. Alyson has talked a great deal about you lately, and I do feel as if I know you. I'm her friend Janet Davenport.'' She laughed, extending her hand toward him.

Chad accepted the handshake and deliberately chose not to correct the misunderstanding. *Jason Michaels,* he thought coldly. *Doctor.* He fought down the urge to blurt out, "And just who the devil is Dr. Jason Michaels?''

"Hello, Janet,'' Chad replied smoothly. "Is Alyson here today?'' Chad struggled to keep the impatience from his voice.

"No, Jason,'' Janet bubbled. "Didn't she tell you that she had the day off? She's gone shopping for a special outfit to wear tonight and to get her hair done. Must be some reception you're taking her to,'' she rambled on. "She's been agonizing over what to wear to it for days now. I finally told her to just get out there and buy something absolutely smashing. Told her I was coming by at six o'clock to check out her purchase.'' Janet rushed on as she saw his raised eyebrows, "Don't worry. I'll be out of there before you pick her up at seven,'' she assured him. "Please come into the TV room, and I'll fix you a cup of coffee.

Most of the residents are having lunch right now.'' She led him down the hallway and invited him to sit on one of the comfortable sofas as she poured two coffees.

"How has Alyson been, Janet?'' Chad didn't know if the question would lead anywhere or if he would get the answer he longed to hear. He just knew he had to ask.

"Better lately,'' Janet replied convincingly. She was impressed by the concern and gentleness in his voice, suddenly thankful that Alyson had someone to lean on. "Of course, as you would know, Mrs. Parsons's death knocked her down for a while. I wasn't sure that she would be able to handle that. You know how much she loved Mrs. Parsons.''

"Yes, Mrs. Parsons.'' Chad felt a great loss. *Poor Alyson,* he thought. *I know how much you loved Mrs. Parsons. I would have liked to have met your Mrs. Parsons.*

"I don't know,'' Janet continued. "The poor kid has been through so much lately. Her father's death . . . and I don't know what happened on her trip to the Yukon, but Alyson was a different person when she got back. She holed up in her apartment for weeks. Thank goodness she accepted that dinner date with you. You've done wonders for her.'' Janet reached across and patted his hand before rising to answer the phone that was ringing incessantly. She had hoped that some-one else would pick it up. "Back in a minute.''

So, Chad thought, *Alyson hadn't fared too well, either.* He was selfishly relieved to hear it.

Janet appeared moments later with Grampa Hill in tow.

"Mr. Hill, I'd like you to meet Jason Michaels—Alyson's friend." She smiled at Chad as he stood up to shake Grampa Hill's frail hand.

Chad was thrilled. "I feel as if I already know you, Mr. Hill," he greeted him, checking his urge to call him Grampa Hill. "Alyson has spoken about you often."

"Sweet young thing, that Alyson," Mr. Hill grumbled as he lowered himself slowly into a nearby armchair. "Just like a daughter to me. Hated to see her so upset over that silly trip she took. Mrs. Parsons's death didn't help matters, either." The old man's eyes misted over as he referred to Mrs. Parsons.

"You the young man she's been seeing lately?" Mr. Hill stared keenly at Chad, a father's air of assessment and disapproval in his glare.

"Yes, I've seen her lately," Chad responded evasively. He didn't really want to tell an out-and-out lie but was willing to allow some things left unsaid in order to push his advantage. He was here to find out more about Alyson, and he darned well would—no matter how.

"Ever spoke to you about her trip to the Yukon?" Mr. Hill asked bluntly. Chad was taken aback at how swiftly Mr. Hill was able to change the subject, posing questions that probed and demanded. Chad wondered what sort of job Mr. Hill had had in his younger years—insurance-fraud investigator? Detective?

Chad avoided having to answer. He hesitated long enough for Mr. Hill to continue his diatribe.

"It was beautiful up there, she said, you know,"
Mr. Hill continued, talking more to himself than to
Chad and Janet. "She loved it. That girl's eyes shone
when she talked about it. But something went wrong,
mark my words. Something went wrong for that sweet
girl. I just know it." Mr. Hill struggled to rise from
the chair, brushing away Janet's attempt to assist him.
"Nice meeting you, young man," he called over his
shoulder as he shuffled out of the room.

"Quite the character," Chad commented dryly as
he leaned forward and set his cup on the coffee table.
"I'd better be going now. It was great meeting you,
Janet."

"And you, too, Jason. Have a wonderful time tonight. I'm sure that Alyson is looking forward to it."

"I can't tell you how much I'm looking forward to
this evening too," Chad replied wickedly, rigid determination in his eyes.

Janet had a vague sensation that there was a double
meaning in Chad's response. She shrugged and turned
to gather up the coffee cups. "Lucky Alyson." She
sighed.

Chad walked briskly along the street, heading for
the florist shop he had spotted on the way. He ordered
two dozen red roses to be sent to Alyson's apartment.

"No name on the card, sir?"

"I think a little intrigue is rather romantic, don't
you?" Chad smiled knowingly at the salesclerk. "No
name."

Back at the hotel, Chad poured himself a Scotch and
picked up the telephone directory. He flipped the pages
to the M section and ran his fingers down the numerous

Michaelses listed there. *Good heavens,* he thought, *how many Michaelses live in San Francisco?* And Jason Michaels. A stuffy name if ever he heard one. He chuckled to himself as he thought of Janet so innocently supplying him with information. He'd have some explaining to do later. Ah, J . . . Jack . . . Jason Michaels, Dr. He scribbled the phone number of the medical clinic on a notepad, closed the directory, and took another drink.

You really are ruthless, Braeburn. He laughed as he picked up the phone. He started to dial the number, then changed his mind. A slight feeling of misgiving asserted itself as he put the receiver back in the cradle; then with a shrug he tore the piece of paper from the notepad, picked up his hotel key, and gulped down the last of the Scotch.

"Hello, Mr. Braeburn. Nice to see you again. How's the Great White North?"

Chad smiled warmly at the receptionist in the hotel lobby. "The Great White North is as wonderful as ever. You should visit there someday. I might be able to repay some of the marvelous hospitality I always get here. In a strictly business sense, of course," he added in a very proper voice.

The young girl laughed. "I'm not so sure I could handle all the wolves there," she said good-naturedly. "I think I'm far better at handling things here. What can I do for you?"

"I would like you to do me a favor. I want to pay a surprise visit to a friend of mine tonight; however, this friend, I find out, has already made other arrangements. I'd like you to make a phone call for me to change those other arrangements. I'd do it myself, but I'm afraid my voice would give me away. And I would like this to be a surprise visit.''

''Well, as long as it's for a good cause and I don't have to tell any lies, I don't see why not.''

''Good.'' Chad extended the piece of paper to her. ''Would you just call Dr. Michaels's office and leave a message with his secretary? Tell him that Alyson has to cancel their dinner date tonight. She won't be home until ten o'clock. She'll call when she gets back.''

A few minutes later he headed for the hotel dining room. The maitre d' was delighted to see him and more than willing to oblige him with his services. For Chad, yes, he would be happy to select the menu. And for a very special lady. His eyes had lit up with delight. It would be a dinner unrivaled in excellence. Exquisite. Romantic. The maitre d' raised his fingertips to his lips and kissed them demonstratively.

Alyson was thankful that Janet had called to tell her she wasn't able to drop by. Her shopping trip had taken longer than expected, Jason would be by in thirty minutes, and she wasn't even ready yet.

She glanced appreciatively at the roses that had arrived an hour ago. Jason Michaels really was a considerate, generous man. Alyson knew that his feelings for her were sincere—and very serious. He was letting her know that more and more. If only she could return his feelings! Maybe then some of the emptiness she felt would go away.

Funny that he dropped into the nursing home, she mused. *I'm sure I told him I had the day off and planned to go shopping. It was sweet of him to go there, though. To see where I work and to talk to the people I work with. Janet had certainly been impressed by him. Imagine anyone thinking Jason Michaels is the most gorgeous-looking creature on the face of the earth,* she thought. *He is nice looking, but gorgeous? Magnetic?*

Alyson had just finished her bath when the doorbell rang. She checked the time. Jason was early. It was just after half past six, and she wasn't expecting him to arrive until seven.

"Who is it?" she called from the bedroom, putting on a robe. She heard a muffled male voice from the outside door.

"The door's open. Come on in. I won't be a moment."

The door opened and closed quietly.

"The roses are beautiful. Thank you very much." Alyson straightened her hair and smiled at herself confidently in the mirror. A surge of excitement had swept over her when the doorbell rang. It had taken her pleasantly by surprise. She leaned down to smell the rose she had removed from the bouquet and set in a single vase on her dresser. It was a perfectly shaped red rose with a sweet, exotic fragrance. Jason was proving to be more romantic and exciting than she had thought.

"Make yourself comfortable. I won't be long," she called through the slightly open bedroom door. "There's wine in the fridge. Perhaps we might have a glass before we go."

Alyson realized her hands were shaking slightly as she applied her makeup carefully. She looked at them in surprise. Her heart, she noted, was pounding at an absurdly fast rate. It was a wonderful feeling, as though the pressures of the last six weeks had suddenly evaporated and left her soaring above her depression. She shook her head in amazement.

"I bought a fantastic dress for tonight!" she shouted, laying the dress on the bed. "I wanted to make sure I look beautiful beside all those prestigious doctors' wives," she commented dryly.

"I'll be respectable in a minute," she continued the one-sided conversation, trying to stop the tremor in her voice.

"There's no rush."

Alyson froze to the spot. The voice sounded so like Chad's. She forced herself to move and pick up the dress. A polite cough from the doorway startled her so violently that she felt as if a shock wave had passed through her body. She whirled round. No sound came from her lips as she stared in stupefaction at the figure in the doorway holding two glasses of wine in his hands.

He extended one to her.

"You look delightfully respectable to me," Chad said, grinning.

Chapter Twelve

The dress dropped from Alyson's grasp. She had waited and prayed for Chad to come, but now that he was here, she found herself rooted to the spot. When he calmly set the two glasses down on her dresser and strolled slowly toward her, she merely followed him with her eyes. It seemed that every muscle in her body had seized. She couldn't move, even to change the open-mouthed look of shock on her face that had locked itself in place.

When Chad came close enough to her that she need only reach her hand slightly to touch him, her hand remained where it was, still poised to clutch the dress that had fallen from it seconds ago. He bent down and picked it up.

"Most prestigious," he said with dramatic irony. He held it out at arm's length, critically inspected it, then tossed it somewhat disdainfully on the bed. Alyson watched every movement as though in a trance. Her eyes rested now on the crumpled material by her side.

"Alyson." Her head turned toward the sound. In the moment their eyes locked, life seemed to flood back into her veins. Still Chad made no move toward her. She was aware only of the power of those coal-black eyes that had bored into hers and held her captive the moment they first met. She saw in them now a mixture of raw emotion: pain, hope, anger, jealousy, desire. Desire or love?

"I thought you were—I was expecting—" The words jerked themselves out of Alyson's mouth. They sounded fragile as they hung in the air between them.

Chad's eyes moved from her face. He looked at the dress and then back at the figure still immobile in front of him.

"I'm afraid Dr. Michaels has had to cancel his date tonight." He spoke the words roughly, as though something were catching in his throat. He made a slight move toward Alyson, then checked himself abruptly.

Alyson sank down onto the bed. "How do you know. . . ." The words trailed off weakly.

Chad walked to the dresser and returned with one of the glasses of wine.

"You look as though you could do with a little help," he said, offering it to her. She took it gratefully, glad to have something concrete to hold.

"Is there a back door?"

"What?" Alyson looked at him in confusion.

"I just wanted to check. We have to talk, Alyson. I am quite willing to wait in the living room for you, but we *have* to talk. I just want to make sure you have no escape out of here.'' He spoke quietly, but there was absolute determination in his voice.

Alyson nodded.

''Good.'' A frown creased his forehead, as though something were causing him pain. He took one last lingering look at her before picking up his wineglass and closing the bedroom door behind him.

The sound of the door closing jarred Alyson into action. The wine in her glass splashed unceremoniously over her robe as her hand began to shake uncontrollably. She set the glass down clumsily on the carpet and wrapped her arms around herself. She felt cold. Her entire body was shaking. She rocked slowly backward and forward.

''Chad's here,'' she whispered to herself. ''Chad's here. And I don't know what to do.''

Her hand brushed nervously across her face and felt the wetness there.

I can't cry. Not now, for heaven's sake.

She got up shakily and took in deep breaths of air. *Ironic*, she thought to herself. *I was wearing this same bathrobe when Chad walked in unannounced before.* For a moment her mouth quivered with an instinctive desire to laugh and cry at the same time. Gritting her teeth firmly together, she pulled the muscles of her face back under control and straightened her shoulders. Despite the pounding, racing sensation in her chest, she walked slowly, controlling every movement. She picked up her glass and opened the bedroom door.

Chad was sitting on the sofa. He didn't rise when she came into the room.

"You're not making this easy," Alyson murmured. She felt awkward and unsure of herself. She looked vaguely around the room.

"Not close to me. Don't sit close to me." The anguish in his voice sounded like the cry of a wounded animal. Alyson moved away from the sofa. She veered round the coffee table in front of it, her gaze falling on the roses displayed there. With sudden insight, she realized they had heralded Chad's arrival.

"The roses are beautiful," she managed to say. "I thought. . . ."

"Presumably you thought they were from Dr. Michael Jason, Jason Michael, whatever way around he presents himself."

There was a catch in his voice. A ripple of excitement passed down Alyson's spine. Chad was jealous. In his dry, flippant manner he had tried to disguise the emotion, but she sensed the jealousy. A flood of hope surged through her. She willed herself not to smile, not to show any sign of jubilation. Chad had come to her; she would meet him now on his terms. She sat down in the armchair opposite him and waited for him to begin.

"Why?"

In that single word, all Chad's pain and confusion showed through. Anything less than the truth was irrelevant now.

"I didn't want your money." Alyson stumbled in her mind for the right place to begin. Chad continued to look at her steadily, his gaze never leaving her face.

"I don't know where to begin. I'm so afraid of saying things in the wrong order. I'm so afraid you won't understand.'' Alyson put her hand to her chin to stop its trembling.

''Why?'' This time there was more of a gentleness to the question.

''I fell in love with the Yukon. I fell in love with you. I fell in love with my father's romantic ideal of love. Everything was like a world of magic I never knew existed before.'' The words tumbled out chaotically, as though pent up for so long, they now competed with each other for release. She took her hand from her chin and placed it resolutely in her lap. She tilted her head up and looked steadily at Chad.

''Kate told me you were the owner of Klondike Enterprises. She thought I knew.'' Her voice still trembled slightly. ''You never told me that. You would have told me sometime, I know. But you asked me to marry you, and you didn't tell me.''

Chad made no comment. Alyson waited for him to respond, searching his face for emotion. It didn't betray any.

''I don't know what I felt at first,'' she continued. ''I felt shocked, angry, confused. And at the same time that Kate told me, I knew I had always known. I remembered all the things you'd said to me about your love of the land, the wonderful relationship we would have together, how much the mine meant to you. You let that slip once. Remember?''

Chad made no answer. Apart from a slight nod to indicate affirmation, his face remained fixed and expressionless. Alyson had never seen Chad in this mood. A swift surge of anger welled up in her. *It's not fair,* she screamed silently to herself. *I'm being made to play the game of my life against an opponent I've never known before. I don't know this side of Chad; I don't know how to handle him.*

"Why do you sit there like some immovable, objective judge?" The trembling in her chin started again, and she moved her hand instinctively to hold it in control.

For a moment Chad closed his eyes. He passed his hand impatiently across his brow.

"I'm not trying to judge you, Alyson." The gentleness in the tone was unmistakable. "I just want to hear the truth. I want to understand clearly in my mind why you took off. Why you didn't give me a chance to explain. I can't give in to emotion. God knows it's taking every ounce of self-control that I possess to stop my feelings from taking over. But what we say to each other tonight is going to determine what happens to us for the rest of our lives. Don't you see that?"

Alyson breathed deeply. She nodded silently. Patiently Chad waited for her to regain her composure.

"Would you have asked me to marry you if I hadn't owned that land? Would you even have looked at me twice in the first place?" she continued. "I loved you so much, Chad." Her voice broke a little. "I almost wished I didn't love you so much. If I had loved you less, I would have stayed, and I would have married you. And perhaps I wouldn't have cared if you didn't love me as much as you loved the land."

She looked away from Chad, taking a few moments to subdue the gathering emotion threatening to break out.

"My father's diaries had such an impact on me."

She turned back to face Chad. "For the first time in my life I understood my father. I understood why he had left my mother and me. And I forgave him. Perhaps that doesn't mean that much to you. You never grew up wondering why anybody could leave you." Her voice gathered strength. "Well, I did. I grew up with an emptiness inside that gnawed and gnawed at me. When I read about my father, for the first time in my life I felt proud of him. I suddenly realized that I had always felt secretly ashamed of what he'd done and that I'd always hated that feeling. I felt free as I never had before."

She looked up at the ceiling and blinked at the tears welling up.

"And you were there. It was like magic. Like I was being offered the same chance at love as my father. A love of such intensity that most people never even dream of." Alyson no longer tried to control the insistent wavering in her voice. The tears trickled slowly down her cheeks. She wiped them away roughly with the sleeve of her terry bathrobe.

"Can you understand what I'm trying to say?" She looked at him steadily. "When Kate said you owned Klondike Enterprises, it was like waking up from a fairy tale."

"You doubted me? You thought I just wanted your land?" The anguish in Chad's voice made Alyson wince.

"Chad, I didn't ask the thoughts to come into my head. I didn't want them to be there. I could have pretended I'd never thought them." The words were punctuated into jerky, broken units. "But don't you see what that would have meant to us? If I thought them then when I loved you so much, how would I have been able to drive them away one year, five years from now? They would have grown stronger no matter how hard I tried to repress them. I loved you too much to let that happen to us."

"Loved? Past tense?"

"Yes, loved," Alyson flashed back. "At least I told you that." She got up from her chair and walked toward the living-room window. The silence hung between them. She turned back to look at him. "When did you ever say that to me?" There was reproach in the defiant question.

"What?" Chad jumped to his feet. "What did you say?" he asked incredulously, taking hold of Alyson by the shoulders.

The touch of his hands on her shoulders burned searing hot. His fingers gripped her like claws of iron. The familiar swooning sensation that passed through her made her go limp for a moment. All she wanted to do was put her head against his firm, strong chest and feel his arms around her. With an effort she inclined her body away from his.

"You said many wonderful things to me, Chad. But you never once said you loved me." The words sounded surprisingly calm.

A look of shocked disbelief registered on Chad's face. The coal-black eyes boring into hers mirrored the sincerity of the emotion. A low groan escaped from his lips. The intensity was too much for Alyson to withstand. She let her body go limp and leaned against him for support. His arms moved swiftly to envelop her. The tension that had kept her rigid oozed out of her as she clung to him, trying to absorb some of his strength. Vague sensations of someone gently stroking her hair and murmuring soothing words floated around her.

"Always loved you. From the moment I first saw you." Alyson strained to focus on the fragments of sounds she heard. She sensed lips brushing caressingly against her forehead, fingers weaving through her hair. Their hold suddenly tightened, and she felt her head tipped back.

"I love you, Alyson Langdon. I love you more than anything else in the world. Is that clear?" The words were unmistakably clear.

Alyson nodded mutely, unable to find her voice. The two walked unsteadily to the sofa and sat down. He took her hands in his and took a deep breath before continuing.

"It's true that I wanted to find out what you were up to when you first arrived in Dawson. Catching a glimpse of that letter on the plane sent my thoughts reeling. That land was important to me, I admit it. I intended to persuade you to sell it. But, Alyson, I fell in love with you, and before I knew it, I found myself in a situation way out of control. I know I should have told you sooner that I was the owner of Klondike Enterprises."

Chad reached for his glass of wine. "That sounds weak. But it's the truth. Every day I tried to find the right words and the right opportunity. But every day it seemed to get harder. When I was with you, I didn't want to bring up anything that could spoil that one week we promised each other. It was wrong of me, but I couldn't stop myself. When you left, I cursed myself for not telling you sooner."

His fingers played on the wineglass stem. "I found out that you'd sold the land because I, too, went to see Jim Dalton that day. I went with what I thought was a brilliant plan that would solve the issue of the land. I was so excited. All I had to do was pick up the papers and give them to you at the Eldorado that night. But everything went wrong. You'd already gotten rid of the land and any ties to me." The words were aimed into the drink that swished unsteadily in the glass under the constant twirling.

"Yes," Alyson whispered. "I knew that you would think I cared more about money than about you. That's why I asked for two hundred thousand dollars. The fact that I got it confirmed for me just how much the land meant to you."

Chad looked at her swiftly.

"I didn't want the land anymore," she continued. "I didn't want your money, either. I wanted you to want me when you had nothing to gain from me."

"That was one heck of a gamble. I think what you did was about the craziest solution I've ever heard. But in a funny way, it was the most brilliant move I've ever seen anybody make." He set the glass down and grasped her hand. "I wanted the land so badly. Then I wanted you, Alyson. I asked you to marry me because I loved you. Because I *love* you," he emphasized. "That's why your solution was crazy."

"And the brilliant side of it?" she prompted.

"I'm not sure if the realization of the two dreams

would have been separable for me if you had stayed—
ever. I never thought of the one without the other. I
thought I had both. But I can survive without the land.
I've found that out over the last six weeks. I can't
survive without you, Alyson. Your tactic made that
brilliantly clear. I didn't have the right to make those
plans on my own. I don't have a right to make plans
for you now. But I do want to marry you. I do want
to share my life with you. Could you see a future with
me in the Yukon?''

''I'm not sure of all the things I want to do. But I
do want to marry you, and I *do* want to live in the
Yukon. The rest we'll plan together.''

''Then I propose dinner at the Sir Francis Drake. It
isn't the Eldorado, but it'll do.''

The lopsided grin that Alyson loved so much spread
over Chad's face. He stood up and pulled her to her
feet. Their embrace was long and tender.

''Shall I pour us another glass of wine while I wait
for you to change?'' he asked.

She smiled in agreement and turned to walk toward
the bedroom.

''I'm sorry about Mrs. Parsons.''

Alyson stopped in the doorway and looked back at
Chad, seeing the concern etched in his eyes.

She felt his sorrow for her and was amazed again at
the complexity of this man she loved so desperately.
This magnificent, unpredictable man she was going to
spend the rest of her life with. *Dinner should make for
interesting conversation,* she thought as she turned toward the closet, deliberately ignoring the dress on the

bed. She reached for the only dress that it made sense to wear.

Chad was seated in the living room when Alyson walked out of the bedroom. She stood before him, love shining from her eyes. She knew she looked beautiful in the black cocktail dress she had worn to the Eldorado. She had released her auburn hair from the confines of the pins that had held it in its elaborate upsweep. Now it cascaded freely over her shoulders in abandonment.

Chad walked slowly toward her. Alyson felt his love for her as he pulled her toward him and rested her head on his shoulder. ''Welcome back, Cheechako,'' he whispered.